THE ELITE

the
ELITE

jennifer banash

BERKLEY JAM, NEW YORK

THE BERKLEY PUBLISHING GROUP
Published by the Penguin Group
Penguin Group (USA) Inc.
375 Hudson Street, New York, New York 10014, USA
Penguin Group (Canada), 90 Eglinton Avenue East, Suite 700, Toronto, Ontario M4P 2Y3, Canada
(a division of Pearson Penguin Canada Inc.)
Penguin Books Ltd., 80 Strand, London WC2R 0RL, England
Penguin Group Ireland, 25 St. Stephen's Green, Dublin 2, Ireland (a division of Penguin Books Ltd.)
Penguin Group (Australia), 250 Camberwell Road, Camberwell, Victoria 3124, Australia
(a division of Pearson Australia Group Pty. Ltd.)
Penguin Books India Pvt. Ltd., 11 Community Centre, Panchsheel Park, New Delhi—110 017, India
Penguin Group (NZ), 67 Apollo Drive, Rosedale, North Shore 0632, New Zealand
(a division of Pearson New Zealand Ltd.)
Penguin Books (South Africa) (Pty.) Ltd., 24 Sturdee Avenue, Rosebank, Johannesburg 2196,
South Africa

Penguin Books Ltd., Registered Offices: 80 Strand, London WC2R 0RL, England

This book is an original publication of The Berkley Publishing Group.

This is a work of fiction. Names, characters, places, and incidents either are the product of the author's imagination or are used fictitiously, and any resemblance to actual persons, living or dead, business establishments, events, or locales is entirely coincidental. The publisher does not have any control over and does not assume any responsibility for author or third-party websites or their content.

PRINTING HISTORY
Berkley JAM trade paperback edition / June 2008

Library of Congress Cataloging-in-Publication Data

Banash, Jennifer.
    The elite / Jennifer Banash.—Berkley JAM trade paperback ed.
        p. cm.
    Summary: When Casey McCloy moves into her grandmother's exclusive New York City apartment building for a year, she must decide if she is willing to give up herself to be part of the most popular clique at the prestigious high school where she will be a junior.
    ISBN 978-0-425-22157-0
    [1. Interpersonal relations—Fiction.   2. Wealth—Fiction.   3. Identity—Fiction.   4. Dating (Social customs)—Fiction.   5. New York (N.Y.)—Fiction.]   I. Title.

PZ7.B2176Eli   2008
[Fic]—dc22   2007052060

PRINTED IN THE UNITED STATES OF AMERICA

10 9 8 7 6 5 4 3 2 1

welcome
to the
big apple

Casey McCloy pushed through the revolving glass doors of The Bramford—an exclusive high-rise apartment building in the Carnegie Hill district of Manhattan's Upper East Side, and stepped inside the cool, gray marble lobby. Casey stood in the middle of the enormous space and looked around slowly, her yellow hair twisting down her back in corkscrew curls that, as usual, went every which way with a life of their own that bordered on psychotic. *Shitshitshit.* Casey sighed in exasperation, dropping the battered blue Samsonite suitcase she held in one hand, a black, beat-up violin case in the other, and pushed her hair out of her face, wishing for the millionth time that she'd remembered to wear a hair tie on her wrist— where she clearly needed it—not packed away in her stupid suitcase. She craned her neck, mouth open, taking in the elaborate colored glass atrium above her head that sparkled in the afternoon sunlight, and streaked the gray, marble floors with splashes of green and gold.

The Bramford's stately marble-and-glass lobby was as hushed and silent as a church, the quiet broken only by the high-pitched, slightly musical pinging sound the elevator made as the gleaming steel doors at the far end of the room opened, and the clicking of stilettos on the marble floor as well-dressed women in clothes that probably cost more than every article of clothing Casey had ever owned in her life combined passed by, leaving an intoxicating spicy scent in their wake. To Casey it smelled like the blooms of rare, hothouse flowers mixed with the buttery-soft smell of leather, and the crisp, green scent of new hundred-dollar bills. Not only was the interior posh and sophisticated, but Casey knew from her relentless Googling, that The Bramford practically defined Upper East Side excess, with amenities that included a twenty-four-hour doorman and concierge—just in case you needed someone to make your dinner reservations at Per Se, or pick up your dry cleaning—a state-of-the-art fitness center with rows of the latest gleaming machines, an Entertainment Lounge on the first floor, featuring an adjacent, heavily landscaped outdoor garden, and, last, but not least, a children's playroom, where Prada- and Gucci-clad mothers could drop their children off before heading off to their weekly appointments at The Elizabeth Arden Red Door Salon for manicures, pedicures, hot stone massages, and salty seaweed wraps.

"Can I help you, miss?" Casey jumped as an older man in a red-and-black uniform approached, his blue eyes kind and crinkled. Casey smiled nervously and smoothed down the white mini she'd bought at the mall specifically for the trip. Her thin, light pink American Apparel tank that had seemed so sophisticated back home in Normal, Illinois, now stuck to her damp flesh and resembled a rag her mother might use to dust the furniture.

"I'm here to see Nanna—" Casey felt her cheeks turning bright red at the mention of the pet name she'd had for her grandmother since she was old enough to talk. And, speaking of talking, was that actually her *voice* reverberating off the crisp, white walls of the lobby? She sounded so totally . . . Midwestern. Not that being from Normal was so terrible—it just wasn't particularly glamorous. "—I mean, *Mrs.* Conway," she said more assertively this time, trying her best to pretend that she'd lived in Manhattan all of her life. Casey wiped a hand across her brow, trying her best to sound like she actually knew where she was going, which, of course, she didn't. "She's my grandmother. I think she's on the seventh floor?" *Ugh*, she thought, pushing her hair back with one hand, *why am I so nervous? And, more important, why do I have to sweat so much?* She'd always hated the summer—especially August. Even her *feet* were sweating in her new baby-pink Old Navy ballet flats. The doorman nodded, his lips turning up into an amused grin under a bushy gray moustache. He placed a large, wrinkled hand on her shoulder, and pointed toward a bank of shining silver elevators at the far end of the lobby.

"Just take the elevator up to 7. She's in apartment 7C. I'll buzz her and let her know you've arrived."

"Thanks." Casey sighed gratefully, dragging her suitcase and violin across the floor, hoping that the delicate instrument hadn't been reduced to kindling during the long, bumpy trip. She felt totally rumpled and gross, her shirt sticking to her back in the humid, late August heat. Just once it would've been nice to show up somewhere looking cool and put-together. On the plane she'd sipped a glass of orange juice, her white Isaac Mizrahi sunglasses from Target covering her eyes, imagining her new life in Manhattan, where surely she'd be as popular and sophisticated as Molly Ringwald in *The Breakfast Club*, her favorite movie of all time.

"But the sexual politics are completely outdated!" her mother would shout whenever Casey put on the DVD for the trillionth time. Barbara McCloy was a professor of Women's Studies at Illinois State and she couldn't understand how her womb had produced Casey, who would've loved to have been teleported out of her own curly-haired unglamorous world, and into the body of someone a lot more exciting. Not that her mother understood—her mother truly believed that making a fashion statement amounted to wearing long hippie skirts in hideous batik prints, and was always trying to get Casey to buy her jeans at Wal-Mart instead of the department stores at the mall—or the exclusive boutiques that lined Normal's small downtown area.

And when Barbara won a grant to do research at some fancy-pants university in London for her first book, Casey jumped at the chance to move in with Nanna for a while. Staying with her dad was out of the question—since the divorce three years ago, he'd moved to Seattle to take a position at an up-and-coming dot-com that had recently folded, leaving her dad out of a job. "More like dot*gone*," her mother had snorted after he called and broke the news a month ago after dinner.

Casey sighed, feeling the sweat coating her limbs. If she were suddenly catapulted into the body of someone truly glamorous, she'd be wearing a tight, sparkling dress, her hair shining in the New York sunlight, men following her down the street like dogs, tails wagging. Instead, she had a juice stain on her skirt, and her hair was full of snarls and sticking out every which way from her sweaty head. Even her bare legs felt grimy—like she'd been rolling around in the street instead of walking on it.

The elevator arrived with the chiming of bells, and the doors opened to the sound of high-pitched giggles. Three girls stood in the elevator clutching towels and tote bags looking cool, sophisticated, and decidedly bored with it all—the three most beautiful girls Casey had ever seen.

"I mean, she looked totally fug. What was she thinking wearing that tutu? I mean, *hello*, its Bungalow 8, not a ballet recital!"

"Totally!" The girl with the black hair giggled, and with that the three grabbed each other's bare arms and stepped out of the elevator, which closed with a loud ding behind them, announcing their arrival to everyone in the vicinity. If nothing else, it was clear to Casey that these girls positively needed an audience.

A platinum blond wearing a white bikini top, a short, pink mini, and hot-pink Tory Burch Reva ballet flats stood in the middle, flanked by two girls—one with jet-black hair, the other a sandy, honeyed blond. The girl with the dark locks wore a pair of cutoff True Religion jeans with her metallic blue bikini, and when Casey looked down, she saw perfectly pedicured toes peeking out from the silver Coach flip-flops she'd been molesting for *ages* at the Coach factory outlet on her uber-rare trips to Chicago. With her gleaming hair and peaches-and-cream complexion, she reminded Casey of the drawings of Snow White in the storybooks of her childhood—the hair dark without being alternative or gothic, and lips as red as cherries in the snow. As a finishing touch, huge chrome sunglasses covered her fine-boned face.

The other girl had hair as honeyed as her skin—which shone against the bright yellow bikini top she wore. Her hair, streaked with golden highlights, was cut to the shoulders, bangs sweeping across one pale blue eye, obscuring it completely. A thin, white sarong was draped across her waist, and a gold anklet shone on the burnished skin of her ankle. Her arms and legs gleamed from a liberal application of the Nars gardenia-scented bronzing oil Casey always slathered on herself liberally at Sephora, but never bought—considering it was almost fifty dollars a bottle.

The platinum blond in the middle was, quite simply, the most beautiful girl Casey had ever seen outside of the pages of magazines like *Vogue* or *Elle*. As shocking as her hair color was, it somehow looked natural, with no roots, and none of the brassiness that usually went along with a severe bleach job. Her face was a perfect long oval, and her green eyes glittered like hard pieces of jade over cheekbones that were sharp enough to cut glass. She looked a little like Carolyn Bessette, Casey thought, taking in her long legs, and flawless golden tan—if Carolyn Bessette were still alive and walking the streets of the Upper East Side . . .

"She's a walking fashion violation." The dark-haired girl giggled, rummaging in her white patent leather Kate Spade tote distractedly, her voice high and sweet. "She shouldn't be allowed to leave the house—much less go to Bungalow."

"Its absoludacris," the honey-haired girl quipped, swiping a MAC lip gloss wand across her already pink, sticky lips. "The doorman must be smoking crack again or something."

Casey cleared her throat and looked at the floor, trying to be as invisible as possible—as if that was ever going to happen considering she was standing right in front of them. She swallowed hard, conscious of the sweat running down her back. The platinum blond fixed her green eyes on Casey and looked her slowly up and down, her gaze catlike.

"Visiting?" she asked coolly, taking in everything from Casey's flushed face, to her stained white mini, and cheap pink ballet flats. "Because you definitely don't *live* here."

"Actually, I do . . . now," Casey blurted out, placing her bags down on the floor and pulling the straps of her tank up on her shoulders. "I'm staying with my grandmother for a while."

"Where are you from, anyway?" the dark-haired girl asked, sliding her sunglasses down over her eyes.

"Normal, Illinois," Casey said proudly, straightening up slightly and throwing her shoulders back. Normal might not be glamorous or sophisticated, but it was home—the only home she'd known for the past sixteen years.

"Is that really a . . . place?" the honey-blond girl asked slowly, her forehead furrowed in concentration.

"Look," Snow White said with an amused grin, pointing at her friend with the honey locks—who looked awfully confused. "She's trying to think!"

"Where's Illinois, anyway?" the honey-girl mused, completely unfazed by the dark-haired girl's comment, checking the time on her black iPhone. "Isn't it near Nebraska or something?" Without missing a beat, the dark-haired girl and the platinum blond cracked up, grabbing each other's arms for support, wiping tears from their eyes with perfectly manicured fingertips. The honey-haired girl glared at them with her bottle-glass green eyes, then turned back to Casey, her expression softening.

"I am *so* bad at geography," she said apologetically, "I barely know where I am at all times."

"You can say that again," the platinum blond snorted, rolling her eyes and shifting her weight from one foot to another, anxious to get outside. "So," she said, regarding Casey coolly with eyes like electric-green ice chips. "*Are* you?"

"Am I what?" Casey asked nervously, acutely aware that she was sweating so hard that droplets of perspiration were likely to start rolling down her forehead at any moment.

"Normal," the blond said with a tight smile. The other two girls had stopped fidgeting, and were listening to their conversation so closely that Casey thought they might be holding their breath.

"I *guess* so," Casey answered uncertainly.

"I would imagine that being . . . I mean *living* in Normal would be awfully *pedestrian*," the blond said with a sly smile. Casey's brain scrambled to keep up with the blond's sophisticated banter—had she just been *insulted*? She couldn't be totally sure.

"I'm Casey," she said, holding out her hand, attempting to navigate the conversation back to safer, less shark-infested waters, remembering too late that her palms were basically an ocean of sweat.

"I'm Madison Macallister, the blond said with an air of imperiousness—as if Casey should've somehow known. "And this is Phoebe Reynaud." The dark-haired girl smiled, exposing rows of brilliantly white teeth. Madison pointed one French-manicured finger at the girl with the honey-colored hair. "And that's Sophie St. John. Welcome to The Bram," she added—almost as an afterthought. The honey-girl waved one hand happily, then attempted to push a heavy sheaf of hair from her left eye.

"Oh my God," Madison snapped, grabbing Sophie's thin wrist. "STOP that!" Madison looked apologetically over at Casey. "We finally got her to grow her bangs out like Nicole Richie, you know—pre-pregnancy? But she keeps fidgeting with them. It's so *annoying*."

"I can't *see* anything like this." Sophie sighed exasperatedly. "I feel like a cyclops."

"You do have another eye, you know," Phoebe giggled, "and besides . . ."

"BEAUTY IS AGONY!" all three yelled out at once, laughing hysterically and slapping each other's hands in high-fives.

"She's just being a baby." Madison pointed at Sophie with one slim, polished finger. "It's not like she wasn't *prepared*. I mean, we made her wear the cutest Christian Dior eye patch for two *weeks* before she even got her hair cut."

"I don't even look like Nicole Richie anyway," Sophie mumbled.

"Not with that ass," Madison added slyly. "From the back you look more like . . . *Beyoncé*." Sophie blushed deeply, and Casey noticed that she was now holding her tote bag directly in front of her lower half and biting her bottom lip.

"So who's your grandmother anyway?" Phoebe asked, pulling out a slim Bobbi Brown compact and checking her coral lip gloss in the mirror. Phoebe looked like she should be pouting on a beach somewhere in St. Tropez, waiting for some cute pool boy to bring her a frozen daiquiri with a tiny pink umbrella in it.

"Elizabeth Conway?" Casey said, wondering why the hell everything she said was coming out like a question today. "On the seventh floor."

"I know her," Madison said, looking over Casey's shoulder and out onto the sun-baked streets. "She's been here, like, *forever*. So, what's that?" she asked, pointing one slim finger at

Casey's battered violin case like a cockroach had just crawled in the front door.

"Umm," Casey stammered, her face flushing furiously the way it always did when she was anxious or embarrassed—and right now she was definitely both. "It's just my violin."

"Are you, like, some kind of child prodigy or something?" Sophie asked excitedly.

"Does she *look* like a child to you, Sophs?" Phoebe quipped, rolling her eyes heavenward in obvious exasperation.

"Don't answer that," Madison said quickly, holding out a hand in Sophie's direction.

"I'm *definitely* no prodigy," Casey answered, looking down at her violin case for moral support. "I've been playing since I was six—but I'm really not that good. I don't even take lessons anymore." Casey was aware that she sounded vaguely desperate—like she was making excuses. She wasn't exactly embarrassed about her musical abilities, but she also knew that violinists weren't usually included in the upper echelons of cool. It was bad enough that she came from a town that was clearly geographically undesirable—she didn't want the first people she met in her building to think she was a clueless band geek on top of it. And besides, she wasn't sure how seriously she even took music anymore, anyway. For the last few months, she'd been contemplating quitting altogether.

"Since you were six?" Sophie said with amazement, her green eyes wide as saucers. "That's like, practically forever!"

Just then Madison's cell phone stared to ring with a series of hyper-annoying beeps and chirps. She pulled a limited-edition cranberry Razr covered with sparkling Swarovski crystals from her Coach monogramed tote, and rolled her eyes. "Ugh. It's Drew. *Again*." She pressed a button on the side of her cell, and the beeping magically stopped. "I'm sorry." She turned to Casey apologetically. "I'm all blown up today." Madison shoved her phone back into her bag.

"Blown up?" Casey asked, her brow wrinkled with confusion. She felt like she'd landed on some foreign planet where everyone spoke a different language.

Sophie rolled her eyes and smiled. "She just means that her cell's been ringing off the hook."

"Is Drew your boyfriend or something?" Casey asked, fidgeting with her stainless steel Fossil watch. She liked oversized watches. They made her feel comparatively tiny and delicate, which was a plus, considering that most of the time she felt like a big galoot—totally uncoordinated in every way possible.

"Ha!" Madison snorted. "He wishes."

"I don't know *why* you won't go out with him again," Phoebe whined. "He's an adorababe."

"Yeah," Sophie giggled while surreptitiously swiping the hair away from her left eye, "he's totally the hotness. He just got back from spending the whole summer in Amsterdam. So, I'm sure he's fried what's left of his brain drinking beers and smoking way too much weed in gross bars with weird Euros in black turtlenecks and high-concept glasses."

"I've got it," Phoebe exclaimed, the corners of her cherry-red lips turning up into another smile. "He's AMSTERDAM-AGED!" Phoebe and Sophie burst into another giggling fit, wiping the wetness from their eyes with their manicured fingers while Madison tried her best to look completely annoyed.

"Oh my God, you guys, STOP," Madison said, finally giving in and laughing along, her relentlessly white teeth shining in her lightly tanned face. She pulled an elastic band off of her wrist, pulling her shoulder-length hair back into a smooth ponytail that fell down her back like a waterfall of silky blond strands. "So," she said coolly, turning to Casey. "Do you know where you're going to school yet?"

"Umm . . ." Casey mumbled, watching as both Phoebe and Sophie glanced at her battered suitcase, then looked away. "I think it's called Meadow something . . . Meadow View maybe?" Her voice trailed off into nothingness. Oh, crap. Why couldn't she remember the name? It's not like her mother hadn't told her at least fifty times over the last month.

"You mean Meadowlark," Madison said knowingly, nodding her sleek blond head approvingly. "That's where we go. We'll be juniors this year."

"Thank *God*," Phoebe moaned.

"Me, too" Casey said shyly, scuffing her flats against the smooth marble floor. Phoebe and Sophie started whispering to one another, jabbing each other in the sides with their thin, pointy elbows. "Well, I should probably go and get settled in."

"We're going over to the park to lay out." Phoebe waved her hands as she spoke, a set of gold bangles tinkling on one wrist. "You should come by later. We've got mojitos-to-go," she trilled, pointing to an expensive-looking aluminum thermos poking out from her baby blue Tod's tote.

"The park?" Casey asked, wondering if there was more than one in the neighborhood, and how to ask without looking completely clueless—which, of course she totally was.

"Uh, *hello*?" Madison snapped, looking at Casey like she was a moron straight from the planet Don't-Talk-To-Me. "*Central* Park? Maybe you've heard of it? It's right across the *street*."

"Oh," Casey said, flushing bright red. "Central Park. Yeah, I know where that is."

"I should hope so," Madison said dryly, "considering that if you go out the front door of this building and walk straight ahead, you can't miss it."

As the trio walked off with brightly colored beach towels bulging out of their bags, Casey couldn't help but feel a little sad as she dragged her suitcases into the elevator. She felt really . . . alone all of a sudden. Her ears popped as the elevator climbed skyward, and she couldn't help thinking about Marissa and Brandy, her two best friends back home. On her last Saturday in Normal, they had wandered around the mall, trying on the evening gowns and lingerie in Saks Fifth Avenue—just for fun, until they collapsed in a pile of giggles in a booth at Starbucks, ordering caramel lattes and gossiping over the latest issues of *In Touch* and *Us Weekly*. Casey felt a lump rise in her throat and her eyes were hot and wet at the corners. Back home in Normal, they were probably driving downtown like they always did on hot, lazy summer afternoons, stopping for ice cream at The Brain Freeze and checking out all the cute guys wearing wifebeaters and board shorts.

Casey felt the tears that were welling up in her gray eyes

threaten to spill over onto her lightly freckled cheeks, and she wiped her eyes with the backs of her hands, smudging the black eyeliner she'd tried to apply so perfectly that morning back in the Midwest. But before she could really start to cry, she stopped herself. *Ugh. Stop being such a baby.* Casey sighed, sniffling just a little now. *You're in New York City—a place where anything can happen. And anything just might! And besides,* she thought with a smile as the elevator stopped at the seventh floor, *I've already made new friends here.*

Well, sort of.

cruel
summer

✦

Madison Macallister lay back on her turquoise and lemon–striped Frette beach towel and scowled into the sun. It was a perfect August afternoon in Manhattan, the kind she liked best. The cloudless sky overhead mirrored the exact color of her new baby-blue Jimmy Choo alligator sandals, the heat blazed through her white Eres bikini, turning her skin an even darker shade of caramel, the humidity hung in the air like the promise of something sticky. Even though most people thought New York in the summertime was the definition of hell on earth, the hotter it got, the happier Madison usually was. But in spite of the flawless weather, the cute guys playing Frisbee in their board shorts, the mouthwatering scent of grilled burgers and french fries wafting through the air, she was in a bad mood and everyone was going to pay.

"Ugh." Madison pushed her D&G shades on top of her blond head, and stared at Sophie and Phoebe—who were busy sipping mojitos from crystal tumblers Sophie had swiped from her parents' well-stocked bar. "Did you *see* her clothes?" Madison shivered with revulsion, her perfect ski-slope nose (courtesy of Dr. Stone, the Park Avenue plastic surgeon her mother positively swore by), wrinkling adorably. "And don't even get me started on that *hair*."

"Her hair wasn't *that* bad," Sophie offered meekly, her eyes hidden by an enormous pair of white Pucci sunglasses.

"Maybe we should rethink your look after all," Madison said with a dismissive snort, lying back on her towel and pulling her shades over her green eyes. "You're obviously going blind."

"Oh, come on, Madison," Phoebe said, removing a bottle of OPI's I'm Not Really a Waitress from her baby-blue Tod's tote, the fuchsia shade winking in the sunlight. "She's not *that* bad. I mean, the clothes are kind of a disaster, but it's nothing a little retail therapy can't fix." Phoebe leaned over and began touching up her pedicure with the bright polish.

"It'll be fun, Mad," Sophie said from behind her huge white shades. "And besides, why would you want to deny me the pleasure of doing a makeover—you know they're practically my only reason for living!"

Madison sighed and closed her eyes, feeling the warm sun

on her skin. She had bigger things to worry about than her so-called friends' imminent adoption of some Midwestern, frizzy-haired loser. She couldn't believe that she was so depressed already—and the year hadn't even started yet! Everything should've been perfect—she was a junior now, and the year would surely be filled with parties, sweaty nights at Bungalow, Pangaea, The Box, and late-afternoon brunches at Pastis with coddled eggs, champagne cocktails, and freshly baked baguettes. The trouble was, she thought she'd be doing those things with Drew.

The truth was, it had been the worst summer on record. After spending three blissful weeks at her parents' beach house on Martha's Vineyard, lying on the beach breathing in the warm, sea-salt air, she had no choice but to leave the sun, sand, and breathtaking water views, and head back to Manhattan to repeat last semester's English class in the most dreaded of activities—summer school—where she'd spent her days reading boring, depressing-ass novels like *Silas Marner* and *Great Expectations*. Adding insult to injury, the air conditioner in her dad's Lincoln Town Car went on the fritz two weeks into the summer semester, and she'd gotten so dehydrated during the six-block ride to school every day that it was a miracle she didn't come down with fucking heatstroke. And on top of ruining what should've been the best summer yet, having to repeat English—which was basically her mother tongue—was totally embarrassing. She wasn't naturally smart like Phoebe or Sophie—not that she'd ever admit it—and if she didn't study, she usually wound up in serious trouble. It had never been a problem before—being gorgeous *and* a Macallister, she could usually talk her way out of anything—but not this time.

Madison flipped on her stomach, burying her face in her arms, momentarily reassured by the scent of the Marc Jacobs Blush Intense body lotion coating her skin. When she was really honest with herself, she had to admit that her life had been a complete mess ever since that warm night last spring. Not that she'd ever confide any of this to either Sophie or Phoebe, but the night before Drew left for Europe everything between them went suddenly, horribly wrong. After two years of breaking up and getting back together, flirty text messages, making out on the floor of her bedroom, two years of lost calls and turning their phones off just for spite, they finally lost their virginity to one another—and it couldn't have been more of a disaster.

The night had started off promisingly. Drew arrived at her apartment wearing a pair of crisp khakis and a white T-shirt, his blue eyes glowing in his chiseled face. As Madison stood in the doorway, her lightly tanned skin covered by a simple Theory sundress in white eyelet, her hormones went into overdrive— all at once she wanted to drag him inside and burn his clothes so that he could never leave. She wanted to vote everyone else off the island of Manhattan *but* Drew.

When she regained what was left of her sex-addled brain, she noticed that Drew carried a wicker basket under one arm, a frosty bottle of Dom peeping out from beneath a white napkin. The air was balmy and warm, and the moon glowed with such ferocity overhead that it seemed to obliterate even the streetlights. They'd gone to the park and spread a blanket out on the soft spring grass, and Drew had produced one delicacy after another, feeding her Beluga caviar and homemade blinis, fresh buffalo mozzarella and cherry-red tomatoes strewn with dark leaves of basil. When she leaned in and licked extra virgin olive oil from his fingers, she wondered if Drew had lost his V-card yet, or if he was still extra virgin himself. And if somehow, he wasn't a virgin anymore, would she just seem totally inexperienced to him? The thought made a lump of mozzarella stick in her throat and lodge there—making her cough like a lunatic, tears welling up in her eyes. Drew patted her on the back until she stopped, his hand lingering on the bare skin of her arms and shoulders. She felt a shiver run up her spine, and an almost overwhelming bolt of excitement run through her body.

Their eyes met and they kissed long and hard, and when Madison pulled back, she noticed that Drew was not only blushing—his cheeks burning with circles of pink—but that he was fiddling nervously with the neck of the unopened bottle of Dom with one hand. Drew Van Allen, *nervous*? She couldn't imagine such a thing. Maybe he just needed to loosen up a bit.

"Aren't we going to drink that?" Madison asked in what she hoped was a seductive whisper. Drew popped the cork with a sound that echoed across the park, and poured the foaming golden liquid into two crystal-stemmed glasses. But before she could hold up the crystal flute to make a toast, Drew had downed his glass in one long swallow and grabbed the cold green bottle for a refill, guzzling the champagne like it was liquid oxygen. "I can't believe that after all this time . . ." Drew murmured, one hand stroking her hair.

"I know," Madison said simply, shrugging her shoulders. "But it feels . . ."

"Right," Drew said, taking her hand in his and squeezing tightly, his blue eyes gleaming in the moonlight.

"Have you ever . . ." Madison asked, her voice trailing off into a whisper. She couldn't believe how small and faraway her voice sounded, or how scared she was all of a sudden that he would say yes. Drew shook his head from side to side, wordless, as she moved in for another kiss, his lips locking on to hers like they'd been doing this forever—which they kind of *had* been.

When they finally made their way back to her apartment and stepped inside the cool marble elevator, Drew took her face in his hands and kissed her over and over, the ground falling away from beneath their feet as they breathed into each other's mouths, her arms wrapped around his neck as she pulled him closer. Madison's stomach dropped to her knees, butterflies swooping and dipping inside her. She couldn't believe she was feeling this way. When Drew had transferred to Meadowlark in the middle of freshman year, at first she'd barely noticed him. Drew was just the dorkily cute guy who always looked like he was in dire need of a haircut, with the weird, artsy parents—until she saw him playing soccer one day in the park. Standing there bare-chested in the weak winter sunlight, his skin still tanned and slightly shiny with sweat, she found herself staring, stopped in her tracks, her mouth falling open. Who knew that underneath all those moose-infested sweaters he insisted on wearing there was a total hottie, just dying to get out? After that, the rest was easy—like everything else in her life. When Madison Macallister made up her mind about something, nothing stood in her way. Of course, it didn't hurt that every guy at Meadowlark was dying to get in her pants. So when she asked Drew if she could borrow his notes from AP Algebra one day after class, he didn't exactly run screaming from the room or anything . . .

In her bedroom, she lit all her Diptyque gardenia-scented candles, stripped down to her La Perla bra and thong set in cream-colored lace, and lay beside him on her white bed, ready to be de-virginized. She wondered if it would hurt, if it would feel anything like wearing a tampon, if she would bleed all over her spotless white comforter. Her brow wrinkled momentarily as she stared at the white bed the color of freshly whipped cream. Maybe she should've put some towels down . . .

When they began making out again, there was a kind of urgency in the air between them that she'd never felt before—she couldn't seem to get close enough to him, she wanted to climb inside Drew's clothes, inside his very *skin*. When it finally happened, she gritted her teeth against the sharp pain, and he smoothed her hair back from her flushed face, gazing at her intently . . . and then his expression changed completely, his face taking on a decidedly greenish cast as he leapt from the bed and ran to the bathroom, slamming the door behind him.

Madison sat up, pulling the sheet around her naked body, which all of a sudden seemed a little *too* naked, and listened to the unmistakable sounds of retching coming from behind the closed bathroom door.

Oh. My. God. This was not happening. Not to *her*. This moment was supposed to be perfect—like the rest of her life. Instead she was lying in her bed, naked, recently deflowered (Did it even count? He only put it in for a minute!), listening to her soon-to-be-ex-boyfriend flush their picture-perfect picnic dinner into the Hudson River. The next thing she knew it was morning, light streaming through the sheer white curtains covering the French doors that led to her private patio—and she was alone in the bed. Madison sat up and looked around in disbelief. The bathroom door was open, the light still burning, but the room was empty. He was gone. She felt like Alicia Silverstone in *Clueless*. What happened? Did she stumble into a patch of bad lighting? Did her hair go flat? Except, unlike Alicia's pseudo-boyfriend in the movie, Drew wasn't gay. Well, at least she *hoped* not. But then again, hetero guys usually didn't toss their cookies at the most crucial sexual moment of their lives, did they?

All day she waited for her cell to ring, checking her messages repeatedly, but as it got later and later her stomach began twisting into tight knots, and she knew—he'd left for Europe without calling her, without even trying to apologize. She ransacked her room looking for a note, anything to explain why he'd just left like that—there had to be a reason, right? Guys didn't just stick it in and then vanish, did they? When she came up empty-handed, her heart sank in her chest.

Later that night, over a platter of salmon nigiri, California rolls, and spicy tuna at Nobu with Sophie and Phoebe, her eyes kept filling inexplicably with tears. She spent most of the night running off to the bathroom, gently dabbing at her green eyes coated in Lancôme's blackest black mascara with a hand towel as she tried not to break down in all-out sobs. She leaned on her elbows, looking into the slick surface of the mirror. Her hair was shiny and brushed back from her face, her skin clear, cheeks shimmering with the peachy-gold gleam of Nars Orgasm blush. What was wrong with her? Madison turned on the faucet as a tear crept out of one eye, sliding down her flushed and powdered cheek. It was their first time—and he didn't even care enough to make it beautiful.

"So, when are you going to hook up with the Drewster anyway?" Phoebe asked, screwing the cap back onto the polish and tossing it at Sophie, who immediately opened it and began stroking the fuchsia lacquer onto her shorter-than-short, bitten nails.

"We're not *hooking up*," Madison said decisively, though she felt anything but sure. When it came to her and Drew, all bets were usually off—then on again.

"I mean, how long can you possibly avoid him?" Phoebe wondered aloud as she lay back on her elbows, her luminous skin shining with a liberal coating of SPF 40.

"As long as I want to," Madison snapped, burying her head more tightly into her arms, careful not to smudge the MAC Lustreglass in Love Nectar coating her full lips. She sighed, breathing in the acrid scent of nail polish and the Clarins Self Tanning Milk Sophie used.

"He's *so* the total package," Phoebe said dreamily, adjusting her wide-brimmed straw hat to further protect her luminous, creamy skin.

"I know what *I'd* like to do with his package," Sophie said with a giggle. Sophie's whole problem was that everything she thought or felt was plainly visible on her open, heart-shaped face—whether she was happy or sad, if she loved or hated you, it was transparent as glass. It was one of Madison's most and least favorite things about her. And right now, Sophie's obvious lusting after her idiot ex-whatever was getting on her last nerve.

Madison sat up, stretched her arms over her head and pinned back her hair while pretending to laugh along, but inside she felt horrible—like she'd somehow slept through the annual sale at La Perla, or lost her favorite pair of silver Manolo sandals. Drew was supposed to be the one guy she could usually count on—so then why didn't he stay and spend the summer with her? Why hadn't they run away to Paris and left everyone behind to live in some garret on the Left Bank, surviving on nothing more than stale croissants and love? Why wasn't he there now, apologizing? Not as if she'd even *consider* forgiving him at this point anyway.

Well, at least not right away . . .

to
grandma's
house
we go . . .

"Casey Anne McCloy! You're finally here!"

Casey winced as she walked into her grandmother's slightly cramped, two-bedroom apartment, sighing heavily as she let go of her suitcases, which promptly hit the hardwood floor like a series of gunshots. She absolutely hated it when anyone used her middle name. It was so outdated and weirdly Southern—especially when it was paired with her first name. Casey *Anne*. It sounded like she should be one of the fringe characters in *Steel Magnolias*. And Casey loathed most chick flicks—she thought they were totally condescending.

"Right," her mother would've snorted. "They're *so* much worse than those celluloid nightmares from the eighties that you're so addicted to." Whatever. Casey had perfected the art of rolling her eyes and stomping off to her room whenever her mother started in with her feminist bullshit—and slamming her bedroom door loudly behind her for emphasis never hurt either . . .

Elizabeth Conway—otherwise known as Nanna—moved into The Bramford in the fifties, and, as a result, the apartment was completely rent stabilized, which meant that she paid a fraction of the astronomical sums the other tenants in the building shelled out monthly. So, after her grandfather's death a few years ago, Nanna just stayed on at The Bram. "Why should I go anywhere?" she'd sputter indignantly. "I have my friends and my clubs. You'll have to carry me out of here in a box," she'd add smugly, promptly removing one of her hearing aids so that no one could argue with her—and no one usually did.

Casey looked around the large living room, decorated in shades of ocean blue and white. White rag rugs were strewn across the blond wood floor, giving the impression of sea and sky instead of granite and steel. Plants in colorful ceramic pots were placed on every available surface. One wall consisted of a series of three large windows—shut tightly—and covered with sheer white curtains. Nanna, as usual, was always cold, and didn't believe in air-conditioning. *Great*, Casey thought surveying the transparent panes of glass. She was probably going to suffocate in her goddamn sleep.

"So, how was your trip?" Nanna grabbed Casey's arm and propelled her over to the soft, powder-blue couch at the speed of light. Sometimes Casey thought that Nanna, at seventy, had way more energy than she did at sixteen. It was kind of ridiculous.

"It was OK." Casey noticed that Nanna was wearing a slightly moth-eaten black cashmere cardigan—despite the relentless heat—and a pair of white linen pants. Her feet were encased in the black Chanel ballet flats she always wore, and a rope of creamy pearls gleamed in the soft wrinkles of her neck. Her straight white hair was still full, chin-length, and brushed back from her face. A pair of gold bifocals hung from a pearl chain, and the room was thick with the powdery scent of Chanel N° 5. Casey loved how Nanna always looked so put-together. "Quality," she would always say, shaking her head at Casey's mostly disposable wardrobe, "never goes out of style."

"Do you want to unpack your things?" Nanna asked. She retrieved her bifocals from her chest and put them on, so that her blue eyes were magnified. "Or would you like a cup of tea first?"

Tea? In this heat? The thought made her dizzy. "Actually, Nanna, I met some girls in the lobby who go to my school, and I told them I might go hang out with them this afternoon—if you don't mind," Casey added quickly. She kind of felt a little guilty that she was planning to take off the minute she arrived, but it was her first day in Manhattan! What was she going to do? Stay inside with her grandmother all afternoon? Not likely.

"Why should I mind?" Nanna said grandly, checking the slim, gold watch she wore on her left wrist. "I have a bridge game down at the club at four anyway."

Casey smiled. Guess Nanna wasn't exactly going to be wait-ing with a plate of homemade cookies every day after school . . . not that she was complaining or anything.

"Let's put your things in your room, and you can unpack later," Nanna said decisively, springing to her feet and picking up Casey's suitcases like it weighed as much as a Nerf ball. Casey grabbed the other and followed her grandmother into the back of the apartment, where it was dark and cool.

"This was my sewing room, until recently," Nanna said with a smile, flicking on the overhead light. The room was small, bordering on claustrophobic, a twin bed with a quilt in blue and yellow dominating the space. An antique mirror hung over the bed, the glass wavy and slightly darkened. There was a small wooden desk in the corner, and oak shelves stuffed with skeins of wool, knitting needles, fabric scraps, and other miscellaneous equipment. *All that stuff is going to fall down on me in the night*, Casey thought, slightly horrified. *I'll probably be impaled on a pair of knitting needles. Good-bye, cruel world!*

The room resembled some demented senior citizen episode of *Project Runway*. Casey half-expected Tim Gunn to come strolling in from the living room screaming, "Make it work, Grandma!"

"I know it's probably not what you're used to," Nanna said worriedly, squinting at the room, "but feel free to put any-thing on the walls you like."

"It's totally fine," Casey said, dumping her suitcase onto the bed, which squeaked like no one had used it for years.

"Well, I should be off soon," Nanna said crisply, looking

at her watch again and moving toward the door. "Who did you say you were meeting?"

"These girls that go to my school." Casey bounced on the bed a little to make it squeak louder. "I think one of them is named Madison?"

"Madison *Macallister*?" Nanna stopped in her tracks and looked slightly impressed, one eyebrow raised. "The Macallisters live upstairs—in the penthouse." Casey knew nothing about Manhattan real estate, but she *did* know that to live in the penthouse in a building like The Bram, you had to be completely loaded. "Well, well," Nanna mused thoughtfully, pursing her rose-colored lips, "you've done very well for yourself on your first day in New York! You're like me, Casey Anne," Nanna said with satisfaction, taking Casey's face between her soft, wrinkled hands and grabbing her chin playfully. "You've got moxie!"

"I guess," Casey mumbled, pawing through her suitcase and praying that there was a least one item of clothing that wasn't impossibly wrinkled. She didn't exactly know what moxie was, or if she even wanted it. She hoped it wasn't contagious.

"Well, I'll leave you to it," Nanna said brightly. "There's a set of keys for you on the kitchen counter. The big brass one is for the top lock, and the little silver one is for the bottom." Casey looked up from the total mess that was her suitcase, nodding distractedly. All she could think about was choosing the perfect outfit for lying out at the park.

"I'm so glad you're here, honey!" Nanna exclaimed, leaning down for a hug. Casey wrapped her arms around her grandmother's comforting body for a moment before she stepped out of the room, her ancient Chanel flats tapping lightly on the wood floors. "I'll be back around seven!" Nanna's voice called out from the living room, and Casey heard the tinkling sound of keys being gathered, and then the door being shut tight, the locks tumbling in their cylinders.

Casey wasn't brave enough to wear an actual bathing suit, and, besides, it would take her all day to find it in this mess anyway. She pulled out a navy tank she'd bought at Express and held it up to her chest. The thin fabric was encrusted with little silver beads around the neckline that sparkled in the light from the open window. *Perfect*, she thought, digging further and retrieving her well-worn, distressed jean skirt from Abercrombie. She'd wear her pink ballet flats, too—for a little more color. Blue and pink could look sort of cool together, couldn't they? And, besides, she really didn't have the patience to dig through her suitcase to try to find anything else.

casey
strikes out

Casey stepped out into the sunlight on Fifth Avenue, the humidity clinging to her skin like plastic wrap. Even from where she stood—just outside The Bramford on the sun-baked sidewalk—she could see couples lying out on blankets on the largest, greenest stretch of grass she'd ever seen. The buildings towered above her head, framing the cloudless blue sky in a blur of cement, steel, and glass that stood in sharp contrast to the lushness of the park across the street. "I guess we're not in Kansas anymore," she mumbled under her breath to an invisible Toto snapping at her heels, the corners of her lips turning up in a smile. "Or Normal."

She walked to the corner, and waited for the light to change before she ventured out into the street. Even so, a bright yellow taxi came close to mowing her down, the cab's brakes screeching on the pavement, the driver leaning out the window screaming, "Get out of the freakin' way, honey!" the horn blaring in her ears as she scrambled across the street, heart pounding.

Even the act of simply *taking* a cab was new—and slightly terrifying. At the airport, she'd waited at the taxi stand in the longest line she'd ever seen for what felt like forever. The driver, a thin, East Indian man with a thick accent, had thrown her suitcases in the trunk without saying a word, and took off through the hazy New York streets like someone was chasing them. Casey had bounced all over the cracked, black leather seats, and rolled down the windows so she could see the skyline she'd been dreaming about for weeks, her blood racing through her veins like electricity.

The park was packed with people throwing Frisbees, lying out on the grass, drinking large bottles of Evian. A small, white dog ran in front of her feet, furiously chasing a red ball. A group of cute guys in brightly colored board shorts—and not much else—passed a football back and forth. The sound of Nelly Furtado and Timbaland blared from someone's CD player. Casey walked around, following the cement path until she saw Madison, Phoebe, and Sophie lying on their towels in the middle of the grass, near a large oak tree, huge sunglasses shading their eyes. Their bikini-clad bodies glistened in the sunlight, the silver thermos resting in the shade. Half-empty cocktail glasses filled with clear liquid and bright green wedges of lime sat on the grass, waiting patiently. Madison lay in the middle, of course, flanked by Phoebe and Sophie.

Casey took a deep breath and pushed her hair back as she approached. She could almost feel her hair reacting to the heat and light, frizzing on contact. She wondered for the millionth time if she'd be better off just shaving her head than dealing with this mess every day. God, she hated her hair.

"Hey guys!" Suddenly it felt totally weird to be completely dressed. She felt so covered up next to Phoebe, Madison, and Sophie in their tiny, colorful string bikinis. Phoebe sat up and immediately placed a huge, black straw hat on her head to protect her porcelain skin from the relentless glare. Madison and Sophie lay motionless on their towels, giggling quietly.

"Hey . . . Casey, right?" Phoebe asked, her voice drowsy and soft. "Come sit down!" Casey noticed that as Phoebe spoke Madison reached out and elbowed her—hard. There was a clamor of whispers as Casey sat down on the grass next to Phoebe's yellow towel.

Madison sat up and pushed her huge, black D&G sunglasses on top of her head. Madison Macallister was one of those girls who would never participate in anything as vulgar as *sweating*. She looked like there was some invisible contraption above her head that just gently misted her all day, so that her tanned skin softly glistened in the light. Casey took in the rings sparkling on Madison's fingers, and the slim, gold chain around her neck that held half a broken heart with the letter *M* engraved on its glowing patina. The heart, Casey knew, was of course from Tiffany. She'd seen Scarlett Johansson wearing the exact same one in *Glamour* magazine that morning on the plane.

"So, Casey," Madison began coolly, stretching her golden arms above her head like a cat. "Where's your bathing suit?"

Casey felt like the intense heat was melting right through the powder and lip gloss she'd applied before leaving the apartment. "Uh, I think I left it back home," she stammered, the lie spreading heat across her cheeks and throat. "I dug through all my bags, but couldn't find it. I guess I'll just have to go to Target and pick up a new one sometime this weekend."

Madison looked down at her own bikini and then flashed her eyes at Phoebe and Sophie, who were taking long sips from their cocktail glasses in an attempt to stifle their laughter. "Target?" Madison said. "You and your grandmother are going to have to get an apartment in Queens if you want to keep shopping there—you'll need some threads to match the address, honey. *Hello,* you're living in The Bram now."

Madison took a delicate sip of her drink while the other girls continued to laugh—only without any attempt to cover it up. Casey just sat there, the heat gone from her face, dropping down to form a cold stone in the pit of her stomach. She looked at the ground, at the drinks, at anything but Madison's cutting gaze, trying to think of something to say. Madison finished off her drink and went to pour herself another, making it clear that the silence was awkward for Casey alone.

"And speaking of which," Madison went on, "how did you get into Meadlowlark anyway? It's kind of exclusive, you know," she finished, her eyes narrowing as she gave Casey the once-over.

"My grandmother knows someone on the board of directors

from her senior center," Casey said, nervously ripping up soft green blades of grass with one hand—grass that was the exact color of Madison Macallister's piercing gaze. The truth was, she'd gotten in on dumb luck—and the fact that she'd been a straight-A student all her life hadn't exactly hurt her chances either. Meadlowlark admitted a certain number of students on full scholarships each year. *Probably to meet some dumb quota,* Casey mused as she'd surveyed Meadowlark's admissions packet three months ago. It was so thick and detailed that it looked more like a novel than an application to attend high school. Casey's mother had faxed the school her official transcript and popped a tape of Casey sawing through Wieniawski's Violin Concerto No. 2 into the mail to the headmistresses, who was, luckily for Casey, the daughter of Nanna's senior friend. The next thing she knew, Casey was holding an acceptance letter in her hands and frantically packing her bags.

"Cocktail?" Sophie said, thrusting a drink toward Casey, effectively changing the subject, the cold glass covered with tiny beads of condensed water. *If only my sweat looked that refreshing,* Casey thought as she reached for the glass, thinking of it more as a life preserver than anything else.

"Sure. Thanks," she said, reaching for the drink and immediately taking a large gulp, then nearly spitting it out as the rum burned its way through her throat. She had never drank much hard liquor before—she didn't really like the taste of it, or the way it went all burny down your throat. In fact, the sum of her drinking experience had consisted of bottles of Boone's

Farm and sips off of 40-ozs handed to her by cute boys at bon-fires. "So do you have, like, fake IDs or something?" she said after recovering from the shock of the rum. "None of my friends in Normal had fakes—you have to go to Chicago to get one—but we'd sometimes get older boys to buy beer for parties and stuff . . ."

"Come on, Casey," Phoebe said, cutting her off. "When you've had a rack like Madison's since age thirteen, you don't *need* a fake. Fakes are totally for fugs."

"Oh . . . fugs. Yeah, I guess you're right," Casey said, desperately wishing she hadn't blown it again. Could she say nothing right? And Sophie didn't look like she was going to throw her any more lines—she was too busy digging through her white quilted-leather Chanel tote, trying to find her cell phone, which was beep-beeping a muffled, high-pitched rendition of "SexyBack"—something Casey clearly needed to bring a bit of herself if she was ever going to compete with The Bram Clan.

"That was Drew," Sophie said, having found her metallic gold phone and spoken into it for only a matter of seconds, "He's headed over to say, 'What up?'"

"Kill me," Madison said with less emotion than a cadaver, pulling her shades down and covering her eyes. "And I was honestly beginning to think that I wouldn't have to deal with his Aberzombie-ass until Monday."

"I know—it's like a miniature herd of embroidered moose make their home on the clothes on his back. He should win an award for animal conservation or something," Sophie said, carelessly tossing her cell in the general direction of her bag.

Casey rearranged herself so she could oh-so-casually drape her arm across her thigh, covering up the formerly tiny moose emblazoned on the hem of her skirt that now seemed larger life. Obviously, the A&F stuff would have to go, too. *I'm going to have to burn my entire wardrobe*, she thought with no small degree of horror. She looked up from her doomed skirt to see a tall boy with thick, disheveled brown hair and blue eyes shot through with red standing behind Madison's head. Casey couldn't help but notice that he had the most adorable dimple in his chin, and that the arms poking out of the sleeves of his T-shirt were golden and faintly muscled.

"Observe," he said mockingly in a terribly rendered Australian accent, "as the rare species of *Uppereastsidiusgirlius* basks in the sunlight of their natural habitat." He squatted down to pull of Madison's sunglasses. "Like dolphins with their love of sex, these are one of the only species of mammals that hunt men and buy clothes *for pleasure*."

He wore Diesel jeans and a fitted white T-shirt, a brown leather bag slung over one shoulder; a hip, modern James Dean for her Natalie Wood with a perm and a decidedly—and unfortunately—more spindly figure. It was lust at first sight.

"Drew," Madison said, coolly turning her face away in order to keep her sunglasses in place, and as she did so Casey got the feeling that behind those dark shades Madison hadn't even opened her eyes to recognize his presence. "When are you going to learn that trying to get a rise out of me is *never* going to get me interested in the, ah-hem, *rise* you get from seeing me in a bikini."

Drew nodded to Sophie and Phoebe, and began to speak again, sans accent, as his eyes meet Casey's, completely impervious to Madison's insults: "I didn't learn much Dutch on my trip," he said, "that is, except for one phrase: *Hallo, mooi meisje.*"

"What's that mean?" asked Phoebe.

"Hello, beautiful."

"Drew, *get over yourself,*" Madison half-screamed as Sophie and Phoebe laughed. But Casey just sat quietly, feeling the shame of her Target faux pas slip away under a wave of giddy delight, for he was still looking straight at her—the pickup line, as pathetic as it might have been, was for her, not Madison.

"So, Madison, who's your new friend?" Drew asked after managing to steal her sunglasses and cover his own eyes with their gigantic frames. "Do these make me look more Chelsea?" he added, as Phoebe and Sophie giggled helplessly.

Madison's perfectly tan veneer was beginning to crack under the barrage of Drew's playful jabs. From listening to only a few minutes of their banter, Casey could tell that Drew knew how to hit all of her buttons, while Madison's image of absolute perfection was tarnished by the fact that she didn't know how to hit any of his. But they did have chemistry—that was undeniable.

"I'm Casey," she chimed in, "Casey McCloy. I just moved in with my grandmother at The Bramford." Great. Why did she say that? She sounded like she was five years old and rolling around in a playpen, a sippy cup in one hand and a pacifier in the other.

"Well, welcome to Manhattan. Would you like a private tour?" Drew said, raising one eyebrow.

"What did you have in mind?" Casey quipped, completely shocked by the fact that she was *flirting* with Madison's pseudo-boyfriend. Was it the mojito? The noxious cloud of spray tan floating around her head and into her nostrils? It had to be something.

"I'll start by showing you around school on Monday and we'll go from there," Drew said, taking off Madison's glasses, perching them on her head, and standing up to leave. "And now we leave this pack of *Uppereastsidiusgirlius*," he whispered, again in the Australian accent, as he slowly backed away toward the cement pathway, "and what an *incredible* encounter it has been."

The four girls remained silent until Drew was out sight. But the silence was decidedly different than the hush that fell after the Target bikini incident. Madison had lowered her sunglasses, but in spite of the way they masked her expression, Casey could positively feel Madison's eyes burning holes in her shirt from behind the smoky lenses.

"Well *somebody* would like to get him some Normal," Sophie said after what had seemed like hours.

"Yeah," Phoebe chimed in, slipping a white cashmere tank from TSE over her head. "And no Abercrombie *anywhere*. Guess he's over it."

"Casey," Sophie said, grabbing her arm and squeezing excitedly, "he couldn't keep his eyes *off* of you. He was completely adorkable!" She turned to Madison, smiling slyly. "I mean did you see him, Madison?"

Madison sat in stony silence. Her face behind her huge sunglasses was impassive, and all at once, Casey's pulse began to race. Madison delayed her responses for so long that it gave the impression that she was—as always—the one leading the conversation, the one in charge. And this subtle reminder was making Casey massively uncomfortable. She took a deep breath in and let it out, furiously searching her pink Coach wristlet for a hair tie—just to have something to do. *Great*, she thought, *I've only been here one day and I've managed to alienate the most popular girl in school.*

"Sure I saw him," Madison said, the words slowly slipping out of her lusciously curved lips as her gaze slowly traveled the length of Casey's body, taking in the Express tank and Abercrombie skirt. "Drew's had a thing for slumming every since he lost me."

Casey froze, her head coming up like a startled deer, her cheeks growing redder by the second. God, she hated the fact that she blushed when she was embarrassed—it made it so easy for everyone who cared enough to look to know just how she really felt. And what she felt right now was the sting of humiliation.

"Oh come on, Madison," Sophie said, coming to her rescue. "Like it or not, she's a Bram girl now. And as long as she is, she'll have to look the part. I only have one word for you, girls: Makeover."

"*Totally*," Phoebe replied, "I mean, with hair and clothes like that, she'll be eaten *alive* at Meadowlark."

Am I even still here? Casey asked herself, pretending to contemplate her pale knees while wishing the ground underneath her legs would simply open up and swallow her.

"Phoebe, honey, I'm afraid you're confused: We're the only ones who do the eating around here," Madison clarified with a smile, the sun glinting off the sharp points of her perfectly polished white teeth.

home
sweat
home

Drew walked home through the park rubbing his eyes, totally jet-lagged, and still stunned to be back home after almost three months. The tall steel-and-granite buildings and the delis on every corner felt totally surreal—like landing on another planet. He could walk in any store on the block right now and buy whatever he wanted. Being back in the land of modern conveniences felt strange after being in Europe for three months—where they didn't even believe in *ice*. But he did miss waking every morning to the slightly muddled and musical sound of Dutch coming through his window.

Every morning he would lie in bed for a few minutes, his mind already racing as he tried to follow along with the broken bits of conversation he could hear from the streets below while debating which museum he should visit that afternoon, and whether he should go to Lisbon or Copenhagen the following weekend. Having decided on a plan for the day and maybe one for the weekend, Drew would walk down to his corner café for an industrial-strength espresso and a marzipan-stuffed S of flaky, buttery pastry. If all else failed, he knew he could run away from New York, school—his whole fucked-up life—and go back to being anonymous. Drew sighed, running his hands through his dark, tousled hair (now standing on end from his overzealous application of Bumble & Bumble Sumotech this morning), mentally replaying the scene in the park, the glacial look in Madison's green eyes when she finally removed her shades. He'd definitely blown it—again.

Drew ducked into a deli, walked to the back, and pulled a Snapple peach iced tea from the fridge, holding the icy bottle to his forehead for a moment before moving to the counter and throwing down a pocketful of loose change. "Hey!" the Iranian guy behind the counter yelled as Drew ambled toward the door. "This no real money!" *Fuck*. Drew sighed and walked back over to the counter. What was he supposed to do with all these leftover European coins anyway? Eat them? Throw them in the boat pond at Central Park? The cashier glared at him, shoving the pile of change across the counter with an exasperated grimace. Drew dug in the front pocket of his pants until his fingers closed around two crumpled singles. He pulled them out and slapped them down on the counter. The cashier snatched up the wrinkled bills, glared at Drew, and threw the cash in the drawer.

When Drew stepped back out into the sunlight, the humidity hit him like a slap in the face. Why did Manhattan have to be so goddamn hot in the summer? And why did Madison have to look so sexy in that microscopic bikini? On the plane to Amsterdam, he'd had all these fantasies about the way his summer would surely pan out. He'd closed his eyes and pictured himself hanging out in smoky cafés with gorgeous, slightly mysterious European babes who smoked endless Gauloises and flirted shamelessly with him over coffee, their red lips leaving behind precise crimson imprints on chipped porcelain cups. It would be just like *Before Sunrise*—one of his favorite movies. He'd buy a Eurail pass and meet his own Julie Delpy somewhere outside of Budapest, the landscape flying by the sun-dappled train window in a blur of green and brown. They'd exchange heated glances in the dining car over a lunch of awful, overcooked steak, and tolerable red wine.

In actuality, his trip turned out to be more like *Hostel*. All the girls he met were definitely gorgeous, but totally fake—they only seemed to be into him because he was American. One French girl begged repeatedly to visit him in New York, and when he said "maybe," she then asked if they might be able to walk to the Grand Canyon—as if this were even remotely possible. She also seemed convinced that America was the Wild West, and asked him countless times if everyone carried guns and wore cowboy hats. And the Dutch girls he met had never even *heard* of Woody Allen, his favorite filmmaker of all time. Just thinking about it depressed Drew beyond belief.

When he first saw Madison lying there on the grass in the park—a spot they'd sat in countless times talking about school, parents, their futures, and each other, he didn't know what to say. Her green eyes were hidden behind those enormous sunglasses that every girl rocked these days—the kind that usually made you look like a mosquito. But Madison just looked . . . hot—and totally distant. He'd broken into that stupid Australian safari routine because he just didn't know what to *say*. Before he left for Europe, he'd thought that if he put enough distance between them, the awkwardness of that night would fade into the past like a bad dream, eventually morphing into something they could someday joke about—like everything else. And the only way he knew how to deal with uncomfortable situations was by making stupid jokes or walking away. Why did he have to be so good at both?

That night in the park, she was so beautiful he could hardly stand it—he thought he might jump out of his skin if he didn't get to touch her. If only he hadn't blown it by drinking so much. But when she whispered in his ear that she wanted him in her bed, he started shaking and couldn't seem to stop. It was highly embarrassing. He thought the champagne would help, but it just made things even worse. What the hell was wrong with him anyway? He'd had a chance that every other guy within a hundred-mile radius would've killed for—and he'd totally blown it.

Drew walked down Park Avenue, nodded at Enrico, the doorman standing at the curb in front of his building, and pushed through the revolving glass doors, the sweat drying on his back with the sudden blast of frigid air. He only started flirting with that Casey girl to make Mad jealous, but the more she talked, the more he found himself actually *liking* her—the sprinkling of freckles across her nose and cheeks, the way her blond hair hung in ringlets around her open, rounded face. And he really felt like he should help her out, being the new girl and all. Drew still hadn't gotten over how much his life had changed when his family moved what was really only a few dozen city blocks. He couldn't imagine what the culture shock would be like for someone coming from any farther away. Coming here from Brooklyn would be like traveling to Mars. At least he had gone from a seven-figure Soho loft to a seven-figure Park Avenue penthouse—it was the crown moldings and the mind-set that was different up here. And she was cute. As the elevator made its way silently up to the thirty-fifth floor, he couldn't help but wonder what she looked like underneath that skirt and weird floaty top she'd been wearing . . .

Drew shook his head, exhaling loudly as the elevator doors opened to a long cherrywood hallway. Why did he have to be so sexed-out all the time? When he really thought about it, there were probably about ten minutes out of the entire day where he *wasn't* thinking about seeing some random girl naked.

When Drew stepped into the entryway of his parent's apartment, he was hit with the pungent, unmistakable smell of curry, and the sizzling sound of grilling meat reverberated through the sleek, modern living room decorated in shades of cream and white. The couch was Eames, and a white, plastic ultra-mod Egg chair sat in one corner, a pair of hidden speakers nestled inside its red, cocoonlike interior. Drew could remember hiding inside the dark, cozy space when he was six, The Beatles' "Blackbird" streaming though the speakers. Splashes of color were everywhere—in the primary-colored shards of pottery his mother had brought back from her trips to Southeast Asia and Morocco, the large, op art circular turquoise-and-white rug covering a large expanse of the polished floor.

The room's focus were the floor-to-ceiling windows that brought in waves of light at every turn, and, of course, the much-coveted view over Central Park, the Empire State Building off in the distance, framed by the Van Allens' enormous, wraparound terrace. When his family had first moved to the Upper East Side a little over two years ago, Drew would stand out on the terrace for hours, marveling at the view and waiting for dusk, that magic time when the sky would soften in shades of crimson, violet, and tangerine, and the lights on the Empire State Building would switch on, bathing the top in a shining glow of light—red, white, and blue on the Fourth of July; red and green on Christmas Day; plain red on Valentine's Day; and electric blue on the anniversary of Frank Sinatra's death. Since the big move uptown, these colors had been the way Drew marked the passing seasons of his life, and nothing represented Manhattan more strongly or iconically to him than that mythic steel spire.

"Drew, is that you, honey?" his mother's high voice sang out, reverberating off of the apartment's enormously high ceilings. From the way her voice echoed, and the sound of

Miles Davis's *Seven Steps to Heaven*, he could tell that she was in her studio again, getting ready for her next big show at the Mary Boone Gallery.

"Yeah," he yelled, throwing his keys down on the Lucite-and-glass coffee table covered with glossy catalogs of his mother's work. Suddenly he was fucking exhausted. He stretched his long arms over his head, yawning loudly.

"Well, come in when you have a minute," she called out over the music, "I want to show you this new piece I'm working on."

His mother's huge abstract paintings and collages covered the walls, lit softly from above by tiny spotlights that brought out the rough brushstrokes in the thick, brightly colored paint she often used—swirls of magenta and aqua, yellow the color of buttercups, lime green and violent fuchsia. Drew didn't pretend that he exactly understood his mother's work, but he did admire it. When she tried to explain her paintings, often times she'd get exasperated, throwing her hands in the air as he asked her repeatedly what exactly a certain piece *meant*.

"Stop *thinking* so much!" his mother would exclaim, laughing impatiently and gesturing toward the large, brilliant canvas. "Concentrate on how it makes you *feel* instead. Drew, baby, your whole problem is that you *think* too much—about everything. It's a painting, not a math problem!"

He had to admit that she probably had a point.

Even if her work was beyond his decidedly third-grade artistic sensibilities, he knew enough about art to deduce that his mother was talented. After all, they weren't exactly handing out one-woman shows at MoMA to every Upper East Side house-wife with a paintbrush and a flair for color. In her twenty-year career as an artist, Allegra Van Allen had had two such shows, to be exact—not to mention countless gallery exhibitions in Europe, Asia, and around the world.

Drew walked over the high-gloss cherrywood floors, for-getting, as always, to kick off his dirty Adidas running shoes, and followed the mouthwatering scents into the kitchen. His dad, Robert Van Allen, stood at the huge, stainless steel Viking stove, flipping the contents of a cast-iron skillet up in the air with a practiced turn of the wrist. His dad wore a pair of jeans so faded they almost looked colorless, with a black T-shirt. A clean, white kitchen towel was thrown over one shoulder. Even though his dad was in his early fifties, he still looked the same as he had when Drew was nine—black hair shot through with gray, and a craggy face dominated by a closely clipped salt-and-pepper beard.

Robert Van Allen had started out a kid from Bensonhurst, who wanted nothing more than to cook for one of the top restaurants in Manhattan. Self-taught, he worked his way up at Jean Georges in a meteoric rise from line cook to grill man to saucier to head chef—all in a dizzying three years. After a four-year stint as head chef at Balthazar, he made a fortune opening a series of restaurants dedicated to providing the Bistro comfort food he loved—French country classics like steak frites, Dijon chicken, and steak tartare—at unbeatable prices. Now, he considered himself mostly retired, and, when he wasn't managing his restaurants or dreaming up new menu items, he liked nothing better than to putter around in their kitchen perfecting some new culinary masterpiece.

"The prodigal son returns!" His dad spoke without even turning around, intent on the meat sizzling away in the skillet.

"True dat," Drew said, opening the stainless Sub-Zero fridge and rooting around inside. Predictably, it was so ridiculously packed that you could never find anything—not that he knew what he was looking for exactly. All he knew was that he hated curry, and he was fucking starving. *An iced tea bought at a deli does not a meal make*, he thought, pulling out some weird leafy vegetable he didn't recognize and zeroing in on a snowy round of goat cheese drizzled with truffle oil. *Score.* Now if he could just dig up some bread, he'd be in business . . .

"I hope you're not planning on eating that." His dad gestured at the cheese with the black plastic spatula he held in one hand, "because I am concocting an Indian feast that would make Ghandi *weep*."

"You know I hate curry," Drew muttered, opening the pantry. He was on a single-minded search for bread—preferably his dad's amazing whole grain bread. He had no time to debate the suck-value of noxious spices. Give him some stinky cheese, some crusty bread, maybe a little red wine and he'd be happy for *weeks*. "And besides, Ghandi was on a hunger strike—he'd probably eat *anything*."

His dad snorted loudly, turning back to the stove and poking at the chicken sizzling in the pan. "Maybe you weren't aware of it," he said, covering the pan with a heavy lid, "but I am redefining the entire *concept* of South Asian dining even as we speak. A radical step forward in the world of haute cuisine is taking place right now in this very apartment . . ." His dad pulled out a crisp *baguette de campagne* from a cabinet hidden beneath the immense kitchen island and threw it down on the butcher block countertop. ". . . And you're telling me that you're just not *interested*?" Drew thought he could make out the beginning of a smile peeking out from beneath his dad's beard as he grabbed the bread from the counter and broke off the tip, smearing the crusty loaf with truffle-infused goat cheese deliciousness. Yum.

"Yeah, Dad," Drew mumbled after he'd taken the first bite, "that's *exactly* what I'm telling you."

"I *thought* so," his dad said triumphantly, sliding the mass of brightly colored chicken parts reeking of curry onto a large, oval serving platter. "Well, don't come crying to me later when you realize your mistake."

"Don't come crying to *me* when you get food poisoning from that mess," Drew smirked, gesturing toward the chicken with the end of his bread. Drew grabbed a knife from the bamboo cutting board and sliced the baguette down the middle lengthwise, then spread the bread thickly with the entire round of soft, fluffy cheese. He reassembled both halves together like a monstrously large goat cheese Subway sandwich. All he really needed was this sandwich, a nap, and he'd feel like a human being again—maybe he'd even figure out what to do about Madison.

"Oh, by the way." His dad arranged two portions of chicken on plates with scientific precision, then grabbed a squeeze bottle so he could arrange the accompanying bright yellow sauce in little squiggles and swirls that decorated the plain white china like one of his mother's paintings. "We're having a welcome home party for you two weeks from today—you know, just you and a hundred of your closest friends. Boudin is doing the catering."

"Great." Drew took a huge bite of baguette and rolled it around in his mouth. This was just what he needed right now. He couldn't have been less stoked if his underwear was on fire. Even the fact that his dad's newest Cajun-fusion restaurant was doing the catering did absolutely nothing to cheer him up. "Do I have to be there?"

"What do *you* think?" Allegra Van Allen swept into the room in a brown and blue batik-printed caftan and a haze of the Egyptian Musk she always wore. A thick stack of gold bangles jangled at her wrists, and bronze, Roman-inspired sandals were laced up her tanned ankles. Her black hair hung loosely down her back, and spots of magenta paint dotted her forearms like measles. From far away, his mother looked about twenty-five, but when you got up close, the small lines feathering out from the corners of her eyes couldn't help but give her real age away. "I'm an *artist*," she was fond of proclaiming loudly at parties when the subject of Botox came up, "not a socialite."

Technically she was kind of both, but Drew knew better than to argue with his mother—she usually won.

"I think I'm horrified," Drew said, shoving more bread into his mouth, his jaws working furiously.

"Well, get over it." His mom smiled as she swung open the

refrigerator door, pulling out a frosty bottle of Blue Moon lager and prying the top off with a bottle opener, the muscles of her forearms flexing.

"Who did you invite, anyway?" Drew muttered, shoving the rest of the sandwich into his mouth in one huge, greedy bite. "The whole Upper East Side?"

"Basically." His mom grinned, her blue eyes sparkling as she grabbed two frosted mugs from the freezer and poured the beer. "And some of Soho, too."

"Great," Drew said glumly. This was *just* what he needed right now. "Did you invite the Macallisters?"

"Did you manage to kill *all* your brain cells in Amsterdam?" His mother's brow wrinkled as she feigned confusion. "Of *course* I invited the Macallisters! Don't tell me you have a problem with that—not after all the time you spent with Madison last spring."

"What's going on with you two, anyway?" His dad picked up the plates and moved into the bright yellow dining room, placing them down on the long cherrywood table where the Van Allens ate nightly—when they all happened to be home, which wasn't very often.

"I don't know." Drew sighed, swallowing hard and running a hand through his hair.

"You don't know, huh?" Drew's dad said, wiping bits of yellow-tinged coconut milk off his hands with a dishtowel. "I know what it's like to not know, Drew. It's tough not knowing, but if there's anything that can help you out, it's the advice of a guy like me who knows what it's like to not *know*."

Great, Drew thought. *Here we go again*. Drew could feel his mother's eyes lock on him the instant his dad began to speak and he knew that if he were to look over, she would be sipping at her drink intently, trying to hide her laughter behind the glass.

"Now, before I met your mother, Drew, when I first came to New York I knew this girl named . . ."

"Marissa?" Drew half-coughed, half-laughed.

"Her name *was* Marissa," his dad said with surprise, sitting down at the dining table and picking up his fork. "How did you know that?"

"Because you've told us this story a million times, maybe?" His mother burst out laughing, stabbing her chicken with a fork and releasing a cloud of curry-scented steam in the air. "Ah, the infamous Marissa . . ."

Drew's dad placed his fork at the side of his plate and surveyed his son calmly. "Are you trying to tell me that you're *bored* of my stories?"

"That's *exactly* what I'm trying to tell you," Drew said, walking toward his room and shutting the door behind the sound of his parents' laughter, and then the unmistakable sound of two pairs of lips meeting and retracting. He shook his head, smiling. He was probably the only kid in Manhattan to have two still-happily married parents—and things could definitely be a lot worse than having a dad who told the same stupid story over and over. Drew kicked a pile of dirty laundry out of the way, maneuvered around his still-unpacked suitcase, and sat down on the bed, grabbing his laptop. He couldn't help but wonder if Madison would someday be one of those stories, if someday *he'd* be the one standing in the kitchen telling his own son about the one who got away.

And as he stretched out on the bed and checked his e-mail, he realized that not only wasn't he ready to become his father, he also wasn't ready to let Madison go just yet.

better late
than
never . . .

Madison flopped down on her white Siberian goose-down comforter and exhaled loudly. Drew had only been back for a nanosecond and already everything was even worse than before he'd left. Maybe now that she was home, she'd be able to calm down—though just thinking about the way Drew had flirted with that horrible Casey girl right in front of her, she seriously doubted it. Was he just trying to piss her off? Make her jealous? Had he suddenly developed a brain tumor? There had to be some reason to explain his decidedly dumbass behavior. Even though Madison didn't know if she even *wanted* to be with Drew anymore, she wasn't sure she was ready to give him up either—especially not to some terminally uncool, frizzy-haired loser. After all, she was Madison Macallister: She had a reputation to uphold and a legend to create.

Madison stared up at the sky-blue ceiling above her head, the only slice of color in her otherwise monochromatic bedroom lair. Her room was the only place in their overstuffed, overdecorated penthouse apartment where she felt comfortable anymore. Her mother, Edith Spencer Macallister, was going through a truly unfortunate Baroque period, and two months ago had ordered the apartment completely redone, and the Danish ultramodern furniture burned. Now, the massive, sunken living room was covered in muted frescos starring demented round-faced cherubs—complete with gold-leaf trim—and the minimalist style Edith had favored last year had been replaced by massively uncomfortable, sprawling antique furniture with way too many spindly legs. Swirling silk-damask drapes in shades of French blue and gold, and tinkling crystal chandeliers hanging everywhere certainly didn't help the space feel less like a museum. All the apartment needed now were a few peasants and a guillotine. Every time she entered the Louis XIV nightmare that her apartment had become, Madison was happier than ever that she had declared her own room with its white-on-white decor, and sleek chrome furnishings, completely off-limits.

A sharp rap on the door snapped her out of her thoughts. Madison sat up and crossed her legs beneath her as Edie entered the room in a cloud of Vera Wang perfume, a bronze Norma Kamali sheath dress hugging her bony size-zero frame, and strappy gold Jimmy Choo sandals on her feet. Ancient

Roman coins spilled from her throat in a shower of gold, and a platinum-and-diamond ring sparkled on her left hand—in which she held a large, cream-colored envelope. Her blue eyes, expertly outlined in bronze liner, were as unfocused as ever due to her chronic pill popping. Edie referred to her monthly intake of Valium as her "therapy." Madison had quit trying to get her mother to stop overmedicating years ago, but if Edie wanted to float through life in a haze of prescription narcotics, then who was she to stop her? They'd played that game for as long as Madison could remember—and she was tired of losing.

"There you are!" she exclaimed, sitting down on Madison's bed and crossing her slim ankles.

"Where else would I be?" Madison snapped, pulling a hair tie from her wrist and pulling her slightly tangled blond hair back in a ponytail.

"I see *someone* forgot to take her Prozac," her mother said with annoying calm, reaching over and straightening the rumpled corner of the comforter.

"Someone around here certainly needs medication," Madison said dryly, picking at a loose thread on her fifteen-hundred-thread-count Egyptian cotton sheets, "but I think we both know it isn't me."

Edie shook her head, the corners of her lips turning up in a smile. "Tsk-tsk," she clucked, "I guess *someone* woke up on the wrong side of the bed this morning."

"I woke up on the wrong side of my *life* this morning," Madison said, her green eyes flashing, "but that's besides the point."

"Well, maybe this will cheer you up." Edie threw the envelope she held down on the bed and smiled, showing rows of brilliantly Zoom-whitened teeth—courtesy of Dr. Haven, cosmetic dentist to practically the entire Upper East Side.

"What is it?" Madison asked suspiciously, picking up the heavy envelope to examine the return address.

"The Van Allens are throwing a welcome home party for Drew," Edie said excitedly, squeezing Madison's arm.

"*That's* supposed to cheer me up? A party? What am I—six?" Madison pulled away, uncurled her legs, and walked over to her dressing room, which had been converted into an enormous walk-in closet. She began sifting through her jeans, looking for her favorite pair of Rock and Republic Stevie jeans with the pink Swarovski crystals on the back pockets. Drew couldn't even act like a normal human after being away for three months—what were his chances of being able to pull it off at this party? Well, screw him, she wasn't going. Not even if he begged. OK, maybe she'd consider if he really begged—and brought her flowers. And Godiva chocolates. And told her that she was right—every time they fought for the rest of their lives. Then she could probably live with it.

"You know, Madison," her mother began in the measured, I've-had-just-about-enough-of-your-shit tone Madison had heard more times than she could count, "if this is the way you speak to Drew, it's no *wonder* that he hasn't been around lately."

"Oh, really?" Madison said coolly, sticking her head out from the closet, her face expressionless, her hands filled with denim. "You think so?"

"Definitely." Edie shook her blond, shoulder-length, heavily blown-out mane—courtesy of Frederic Fekkai—vigorously for emphasis. She loved helping Madison with her boy problems; it made her feel as though she was fulfilling some great maternal duty.

"He hasn't been around because HE'S BEEN IN AMSTERDAM FOR THE WHOLE SUMMER!" Madison screamed, finally losing what was left of her patience, and throwing the armload of jeans on the floor as her MacBook erupted in a jangling of bells.

"Amsterdam," Edie mused thoughtfully, examining her glossy, French-manicured nails. "Hmm. When did he get *back*?"

Madison rolled her eyes, walked over from the closet and sat down at her desk, logging on to Gchat. "Today, Mother. He got back *today*." Madison turned around and pointed to the invitation laying on the bed. "Hence the need for a *welcome home party*." God, why didn't her mother take the hint and just leave? Every time Edie attempted any kind of mother/daughter bonding, it was always a disaster. Most of the time, it was hard for Madison to believe that she and her mother were even remotely related, much less mother and daughter.

"Well," Edie said brightly, "I'm sure you have your hands full with the first day of junior year coming up so quickly." She got up, absentmindedly smoothing the material of her dress with the palm of one hand. Edie walked toward the door, then paused, motionless for a moment, one hand on the knob. "It *is* Monday, isn't it?"

Madison rolled her eyes so hard it felt as if they might get stuck there and start rattling around in her skull. "Yes, Mother, school starts Monday."

"I *knew* it," Edie said triumphantly, closing the door behind her.

Madison shook her head as she checked her e-mail, deleting a shitload of spam from her inbox. She couldn't exactly blame her father for running for the hills last year. Living with Edie was like living in the fucking looney bin. But having a father you saw on the first Sunday of every month—if he didn't cancel—was like having no father at all. Madison didn't know exactly what it was that her dad did for a living—something with finance, maybe? But whatever it was, it kept him preoccupied enough with fifteen-hour workdays and chronic overtime. Even before the divorce, she'd gotten used to not really having a two-parent household. Even on the rare occasions when her father had been home, he'd immediately locked himself in his office and yelled at people on the phone all night long.

The computer sounded again, signaling an instant message.

dva1990: "Of all the computers, on all the networks, in all the world, she had to walk into mine . . ."

Madison smiled, despite her anger. Drew knew that *Casablanca* was the only "old" movie that she loved. In fact, it was the only movie they'd ever been able to agree on—usually she thought anything in black-and-white was outdated and boring. On their first real date, he'd taken her to a midnight showing at the Angelika, and they'd sat in the darkness, both mouthing every word along with Bogie and Bergman.

> socialiez666: Um, technically aren't you walking into *mine*?
> dva1990: Good point. ☺
> dva1990: Sorry about today. U have plans for breakfast tomorrow?

Madison smiled as her fingers flew across the keyboard.

> socialiez666: Care to make me an offer I can't refuse?
> dva1990: You know the place, you know the time, but just in case—Uncommon Grounds, 10 AM? Be there?
> socialiez666: Definitely. ☺

Madison logged off and leaned back in her chair, smiling happily. What an idiot she'd been to think that Drew was even remotely interested in anyone else. After all, there was only one Madison Macallister, and everyone wanted her. It would only be a matter of time before she had Drew back just where she wanted him—and then she could decide what to do next. She looked at her overstuffed closet, wondering what to wear. She needed an outfit that would make him drop to his knees when she walked through the door. A flounce of blue-and-white tropical-printed silk caught her eye. She was still mad at Drew, of course, but that didn't mean that she had to punish her new Tracey Feith sundress, did it?

sibling
rivalry

Sophie St. John stared into the enormous Viking refrigerator in her parents' apartment in The Bramford, completely and utterly confused. She could've *sworn* that she had a leftover spicy tuna roll from Nobu in here yesterday. Their maid, Marguerite, had left Sophie her usual daily snack of chilled raw carrots and celery sticks on a white Spode dinner plate. But Sophie didn't want carrots—she wanted a spicy tuna roll. Ever since Madison had embarked on her turn-Sophie-into-Nicole Richie plan, she'd been trying to lose five pounds—not that it was going very well with all the mojitos she'd drank today. Where the hell was that spicy tuna roll, anyway? Sophie kicked off her pink Coach flip-flops and flexed her bare feet on the cool, Mexican-tiled floor. She leaned over and rummaged in the back of the fridge, digging behind some moldy lettuce. She was going to go seriously psychotic if she didn't find that sushi.

"Find anything interesting?"

Sophie turned around to face her older (by one year—not that he ever stopped yakking about it) brother, Jared, who had entered the kitchen wearing green Billabong board shorts and a black T-shirt. Jared had the body of a swimmer—all tanned flesh and lean muscle, and was forever planning complicated surfing expeditions to Hawaii or the Great Barrier Reef in Australia. He already had plans to move out to Southern California next year so he could surf full-time. And considering that he just got kicked out of Exeter at the start of his senior year, it seemed as good an option as any. Not that anyone was talking about it. Her parents—and Jared for that matter—had been decidedly tight-lipped about the details surrounding his expulsion. All Sophie knew was that for the last two years she'd basically had the run of their immense apartment, and now that Jared was back, not only did he *always* seem to be home, but to add insult to injury, her food also began disappearing on a regular basis—something that really annoyed her. Despite her size-two figure, or maybe because of it, the one thing Sophie really loved was her food. Steal it and you were going to pay—big-time.

Sophie rolled her eyes as she took in her brother's greasy hair and rumpled, dirty clothes. Jared was truly the king of multislacking, and, as a result he'd perfected the fine art of whiling his days away surfing the Web, watching random TV shows, and text messaging his loser friends—all at the same time. His greasy dark hair fell over one blue eye, and Sophie noticed immediately that he was chewing on something that smelled suspiciously fishy.

Sophie stood up, hands on her hips, her cheeks flushed with two burning circles of red. "That better not be *my* spicy tuna roll you're stuffing in your face!"

Jared swallowed hard, his full, red lips stretching into a grin. "First come," he said, flopping down on one of the supremely uncomfortable wooden chairs their mother had insisted on, and put his tanned, bare feet up on the shiny oak dining table, "first served." Jared smiled, placing his hands behind his head and leaning back in his chair. Just looking at his smug, self-satisfied face made Sophie want to punch him—so she did just that.

"Ow!" Jared yelled after her fist had made contact with his washboard abs, "calm down, will you? It was just *sushi*."

"*My* sushi," Sophie yelled, pointing at her chest with an index finger. "Why are you always stealing my food?"

"What did you have for breakfast this morning?" Jared asked irritably. "Hater tots? And why are you so hung up on labels? Mine, yours?" Jared's face was plastered with that holier-than-thou expression that drove her absolutely nuts. "We *are* a family, you know," he said, looking her up and down, taking in her blond hair and burnished skin, courtesy of Mystic Tan. "Even if you *are* the only living proof that Mom's had an affair." Jared arched one dark brow, reaching out to pinch his sister's leg. Hard.

"Ow!" Sophie yelled as his fingers made contact and twisted her slightly sunburned thigh.

"Payback's a bitch," Jared said airily, standing up and stretching his arms overhead, then he shuffled out of the room and down the hall to his bedroom, humming the new Fallout Boy song under his breath, just to annoy her. She hated Fallout Boy.

Sophie opened the fridge and looked inside again, then slammed the door, leaning against the cold fridge, crossing her arms over her chest. As she stood there, thinking that she should just order Chinese, Sophie wondered why she always felt like an outsider, even in her own home. With her honey-blond hair, skin that positively screamed for self-tanner, and light green eyes, Sophie couldn't have looked less like an alien from space next to her tall, dark-haired family. Her parents, Alistair and Phyllis St. John, were both blessed with olive skin that tanned easily—just like Jared—while Sophie was small and resolutely, blandly blond, and, as a result, totally dependent on spray tans and level-50 sunblock.

Sophie knew that every teenager probably felt like an imposter around their family, but people had literally been stopping Phyllis on the street since Sophie was born and asking if she was adopted. "Oh, what a cute baby," some Upper East Side robot would coo, waggling her jeweled fingers in Sophie's carriage. "Is she *yours*?" Over the years, it had become something of a family joke—especially to Jared, who never tired of pointing out the fact that Sophie resembled Madison more than her own family. After a while, Sophie gave up and started tanning zealously—just so there wouldn't be so many annoying questions. She's even thought about dying her hair, but Madison told her she'd look totally washed-out as a brunette, and Sophie, after a few nights staring into the mirror with a black T-shirt over her head to simulate hair, had to admit that, as usual, Madison was probably right.

Sophie walked over to the pantry, grabbed an almost-empty box of Jared's Cap'n Crunch and sat down at the kitchen table, digging her hand in the box and shoving a handful of the sugary cereal into her mouth. Payback *was* a bitch. As she chewed, she turned over her wrist, examining the faint white scars that streaked across her skin, running her fingers across the raised flesh. When she felt really bad or overwhelmed, it helped to cut herself—just a little. Sometimes she used a kitchen knife, sometimes a blade she pulled from her father's razor. Sophie knew that it was wrong, and she always stopped when she saw the blood running over her wrist, staining her skin crimson. The shock of red was like waking out of a bad dream, and afterward, as she bandaged the wound, cleaning the cut out with hydrogen peroxide, the sting of the antiseptic, the clutch of the white bandage was always strangely, calmly reassuring.

When Phoebe and Madison finally noticed the scratches one day last fall during a nostalgic-for-their-youth moment at Serendipity 3 over frozen hot chocolate, Sophie had to think fast. "It's Snowball," she had said, blushing and stuttering as usual, "she gets so excited when we play." Just then Snowball, a fluffy white Persian, slunk into the kitchen and meandered over to her water bowl, lapping at the water delicately with her small, pink tongue. Sophie watched her kitty drink and wondered how long her friends would continue to believe her—assuming they did already—if she kept cutting. As it was, Madison surveyed any fresh marks with a lethal combination of raised, perfectly waxed eyebrows, and steely silence . . .

Her last shrink, Dr. Breuer, a dark-haired woman in her forties who wore the same pair of black pants every week—even though she charged two hundred and fifty dollars a session—diagnosed Sophie with ADD and prescribed Adderall, which made Sophie feel screamingly productive, but kind of spacey, too. "Try to focus on something or someone else when you have the urge to self-mutilate, Sophie," she'd said, peering over her hideous horn-rimmed glasses. Sophie hated that expression—*self-mutilate*—it sounded so . . . serious. At least she wasn't out all night long smoking crack. And it wasn't like she cut herself every day or anything—just when things got, well, a little too *much*. Sophie wrinkled her forehead and leaned her elbows on the table, pushing the cereal box aside, her palms resting under her chin.

Maybe they should go shopping tomorrow. After all, Casey could really use all the help she could get if she didn't want to be crucified on her first day at Meadowlark, and there was nothing that Sophie liked better than doing a makeover. Casey would probably even be pretty if they did something with that fugly-ass hair and got her some decent clothes. Besides, Monday was the first day back at school, and as Sophie mentally Rolodexed her closet, she realized she had absolutely nothing to wear. She was in desperate need of the perfect outfit—one that screamed confidence, style, and sophistication—in the most understated way possible, of course. Grabbing her phone from the table, she texted Phoebe, her fingers moving rapidly across the keypad.

What up?
Nada. You?
Shopping tomorrow? Casey needs help! MAKEOVER!
Sure . . . but . . .

Sophie frowned at the colorful display screen of her iPhone. When she'd bought it six months ago, her father had actually yelled at her for the first time ever when he got the bill. "Four hundred dollars for a *phone*, Sophia?" he demanded, his face turning the same shade of salmon pink as the Hermès silk tie knotted at his throat. "What's it made out of—rare, imported, gold-plated titanium?"

"Oh, please, Alistair," her mother had snapped, coming to Sophie's rescue. "Let me remind you that I spend more money on a single pair of shoes—and I don't hear you hollering about *that*."

"I might, if I thought it would do any good," her dad mumbled, throwing his hands in the air in frustration and walking out of the room

The screen stayed blank, and Sophie sighed impatiently. Phoebe loved shopping the way junkies loved heroin—so what was the problem? Actually, when Sophie stopped to think about it, there probably wasn't much of a difference between the two—shopping was definitely a drug, not to mention one hell of an addiction. And Sophie intended on getting high to-morrow if it was the last thing she did . . .

There was a brief pause, and then the phone lit up again with Phoebe's nervous reply.

Mad's not going to like it . . .

Maybe not, Sophie thought, the corners of her lips turning up in a smile. But that didn't necessarily mean they shouldn't do it . . . did it? As far as Sophie was concerned, the fact that Mad would probably be totally livid meant they should *definitely* do it. *Why,* she wondered as she texted back, *does it feel so good to be so bad?*

Barney's at noon?
K. ☺

Sophie turned her phone off and dug her hand back into the box, grabbing the last handful of sugary cereal and popping it in her mouth, chewing contentedly—the diet, Madison, and the scars on her wrist momentarily forgotten.

boys . . . they're not just for breakfast anymore

Madison stood in the open doorway of Uncommon Grounds, her navy-and-white, Tracy Feith sundress swirling around her legs in the morning breeze. She walked into the coffee shop/restaurant, inhaling the tantalizing scent of roasting beans and freshly baked flaky pastries, pushing her hair from her shoulders with one hand while clutching her navy-and-white Fendi B bag with the other. The room was crowded with early-bird New Yorkers crouched over lattes, plates of free-range eggs, thick-cut organic bacon, and plump blueberry streusel muffins, the classic gray Formica-topped tables pushed up against bright yellow walls.

Uncommon Grounds had always been *their* place—the scene of countless fights and make-up breakfasts, late-night cups of ginger tea, and long talks over eggs Benedict and milky café au lait. It was where she and Drew had first held hands under the cramped table two summers ago, his fingers tentatively stroking her palm while Phoebe and Sophie bickered endlessly about how many fat grams were in a single brioche.

She craned her neck slightly until she spied Drew at a tiny table in the back of the room, a framed poster of an oversized coffee mug directly over his head. In his ancient olive cargos and black American Apparel T-shirt, he wasn't exactly dressed to impress, but Madison thought he'd never looked cuter, even totally jet-lagged and moodily staring into his coffee, a decimated copy of the *New York Times* spread out in front of him. As she stared, she couldn't help remembering all the fun they'd had last year—the movies they'd rented on random Saturday nights when there was nothing else to do, how he'd held her close as they sweated under the lights sweeping across the dance floor at Marquee. Just looking at him sitting there waiting for her, she finally admitted to herself just how much she'd missed him while he'd been away—and how much she might want him back.

Madison took a deep breath, forcing her white Dolce sandals to move forward. It wasn't like the two of them ever had much in common—other than being beautiful, that is. Madison hardly expected Drew to be the house-in-the-Hamptons type of guy. She had never imagined marrying anything less than royalty. But now, watching the way a lock of dark hair fell over his forehead, she wasn't so sure anymore. *What if I was wrong*, she thought, her brow crinkling. *What if*

Drew really is the one? And then an infinitely more terrifying thought crossed her mind, and her pulse began to race, her heart beating loudly underneath her lavender Agent Provocateur bra, her stomach dropping to somewhere around her ankles.

And what if he just isn't interested anymore?

Just then Drew lifted his gaze from his cup and looked across the room, meeting her eyes. Immediately Madison forced her face into a dazzling smile and raised one hand in greeting. *You're being ridiculous*, she told herself as she crossed the room, her long legs moving purposefully, confidence regained. After all, she'd practically made a career out of getting exactly what she wanted, from *anyone* she wanted. Why should Drew be any different?

Drew's formerly sullen face broke into a wide grin as she maneuvered around the tables and chairs, and approached the cluttered table. He looked so goddamn cute that she wanted to shove the newspaper to the floor, throw him on top of the table, and force him to make out with her until they were both gasping for air. That would give Arts and Leisure a whole new meaning—not that she ever made it past the Style section . . .

But first things first. She needed coffee. Stat.

Madison sat down across from Drew, her knees bumping into his long legs beneath the table. Drew started gathering up the crumpled newspapers that surrounded them—so much potential history in sticky black ink—as the waitress approached, leaning down to take Madison's order.

"I'll have a skinny vanilla latte with an extra shot," she said, smiling across the table at Drew, who stared into her green eyes, grinning back. All at once she remembered that she was still mad at him: The last time they really saw each other he'd left her naked in her bed, and he hadn't even really apologized yet! He owed her a fucking *litany* of apologies. Losing her virginity was a moment she would never forget—and that memory wasn't what it should have been. Why should she make it easier for him? Madison's eyes narrowed further as the waitress shifted her weight impatiently.

"To *go*."

The waitress scribbled something unintelligible on her pad and walked away, the smile sliding from Drew's face like evaporating foam on a cappuccino. "So, you're leaving already?" he said, one eyebrow arched. "You just *got* here."

"True." Madison dropped her bag on the floor and pushed the wadded-up sports section to the side. "But I think we both know that you'll probably start pissing me off in a mere moment."

"Touché," Drew said, leaning back in his chair and running a hand through his already hopelessly tousled hair, causing it to stand on end in that cluelessly adorable way that made her want to climb into his lap and stay there. What the hell was going on with her? And why was it so hard to stay mad at him? Until he showed up yesterday at the park she was positively fuming, and now . . . now she didn't know how she felt— except that she was completely confused.

"So," she said coolly, leaning forward on her elbows, "how was your summer?"

"It was good, I guess." Drew took a gulp of his coffee, grabbed a sugar packet, and dumped the contents into his half-empty cup. "The coffee here tastes like piss in comparison." Madison smiled, remembering that Drew liked his coffee totally fagged out—with tons of cream and sugar. "My home base was Amsterdam, but I backpacked around a lot."

"I bet you met a ton of people." *Especially ones with vaginas*, she thought, trying to push her face into a smile and look interested.

"I met a few," Drew said offhandedly, pushing his hair off his face, exposing his lightly stubbled jaw. "I met this girl in Barcelona—her name was Eva. Anyway, I ran into her at a café on the Ramblas, and she gave me a private tour of the city."

Of course she did. Madison felt like her blood was steaming in her veins. Her ice-green eyes narrowed until they were practically slits, the color matching the sudden wave of jealousy coursing through her. What was he trying to do—give her an aneurysm? She tried to compose herself. It would totally suck to lose her cool so early in the conversation. *So he hung out with some Eurotrash skank all summer. Big deal. After all, I'm me—and I'm here.*

Madison looked down at her nails, painted with Chanel's Black Satin polish—the choice for Upper East Side prep school girls gone bad—and contemplated her options. One: She could throw down her chair and storm off, slamming the café door behind her with a satisfying clamor of bells. Two: She could reach across the table and smack Drew, insensitive fuckhead that he was, full on in the face. Or three: She could do what she did best and steer the conversation back to the only subject really worth talking about—herself. Didn't he care about her summer, or what *she'd* been doing? And was he ever going to apologize for the way he'd behaved before he left?

At this point, she wasn't exactly holding her breath.

"So, my summer was . . . really weird," she began, just as the waitress arrived with her latte. "I'm still getting used to my dad not being around anymore." She took a sip of her latte before continuing. "And plus I had to spend most of the last six weeks in summer school—which was a complete suckfest, by the way. Not recommended."

"Speaking of school," Drew said, taking a slug of his coffee, which was probably ice-cold by now, "what's the deal with that Casey chick you were hanging with in the park yesterday?"

Madison grabbed her cup, staring at him over the plastic rim. Was he fucking kidding? Here she was trying to get real with him about her screwed-up family life, and her horrendous summer locked in a stuffy classroom, and all he wanted to talk about was some frizzy-haired loser! Wasn't he even going to mention the fact that he was, umm, *inside* her the last time they saw each other?

"Is that really what you want to talk about, Drew? Some frizzfest from the Midwest?" Madison spat back.

"Whoa, Mad. I was just *asking*." Drew said, leaning back from the table as if the ferocity in Madison's voice had pushed him physically. "Is small talk off limits with you today or something?"

"Why don't we just cut to the chase, *Andrew*." Drew's face went blank, and he stared down at the tabletop like it was the most fascinating thing he'd ever seen.

"I don't know what you're talking about," he mumbled, one finger tracing patterns in a spilled drop of mocha-colored coffee. Just then, the waitress—with the impeccable timing and the warped sixth sense of all servers—made the mistake of approaching their table, clearly unaware of the brewing intensity of their conversation.

"Can I get you two anything else?" she said, toying with her pencil and paper as she—as Madison saw it—obviously gave Drew the once-over.

"I think we're fine," Drew said, "but can I ask you something? Why is it that the coffee here is so, well, *different*. I mean, I just got back from a summer spent in Amster—"

"YOU'VE GOT TO BE KIDDING ME," Madison screamed, throwing a five down on the table. The other diners turned around in their chairs, mild expressions of amusement crossing their faces. This was Manhattan, and stranger things than a couple having a random, caffeine-fueled blowout on a Sunday morning happened every day of the week. Madison stood up and faced the waitress, grabbing her bag. "Actually," she said, her voice like honey spread on steel, "you can bring *him* a fucking shovel." She pointed at Drew, who looked like he'd just been smacked in the face with a two-by-four. *Don't tempt me*, she thought. *Just don't fucking tempt me.* "He's going to *need* it to dig himself out of the hole he's currently in."

As she stomped out of the restaurant, into the humid

August air and walked slowly down the street, hot tears blurred her vision, smearing the navy Urban Decay liquid liner she'd applied so hopefully an hour ago. Madison couldn't help looking over her shoulder as she walked, half hoping that Drew would run out of the restaurant and tell her to wait, that he was sorry, that he'd missed her when she was gone. Not that she would forgive him after the way he treated her today. She wanted *something* to happen just so things wouldn't end this way—with her crying on the crowded streets of Manhattan, ruining her new shoes on the hot pavement and smearing her fucking eye makeup.

But, a block later, she'd twisted her ankle twice, and the only thing telling her to halt was the stoplight at the corner of Park and Ninety-first as it changed ominously from green to red.

shut out
and
shot down

Drew watched open-mouthed as Madison walked briskly to the front door of the restaurant, slamming it behind her. The waitress stood there motionless, the coffee carafe in the air, her passing hand halted over Drew's empty cup.

"Wow," she said, one blond eyebrow raised, "I guess she told you." The amusement in her voice was almost more than Drew could take at that particular moment, and he shot her an annoyed look as he waited for a refill. He was never going to get through this morning without more coffee. Ever since Amsterdam, he'd developed a serious caffeine addiction. *More like psychosis,* he thought, replaying his stupid comment to the waitress that sent Madison running for the door. Maybe he should just get an IV inserted into his goddamn arm and start taking it intravenously . . .

The waitress leaned over, the wrinkles around her blue eyes softening as she took in Drew's obviously miserable face. "So, do you want anything else this morning?" she asked, shooting Drew a look of pity as she refilled his cup to the brim. "Or have you had enough?"

"Enough," Drew mumbled, exhaling loudly. The waitress nodded and walked away before Drew could say anything else.

Drew tipped the silver pitcher of cream into the dark liquid until it lightened to a pale mocha. What had happened? He wished he could rewind the day and start over. It wasn't even noon yet and he'd already screwed things up. Drew dumped four packets of raw sugar into his coffee, stirring the steaming liquid contemplatively. When he woke up this morning, he'd had it all planned out. He'd meet Madison for breakfast like they did every Sunday, and he'd apologize—really apologize—for the way he'd handled things the last time they were together.

He wasn't sure how it happened, but when she walked in, backlit by the morning sunlight, that barely-there sundress swirling around her sun-kissed arms and legs, her hair a perfectly groomed blond mane—he went a little crazy. And before he could stop himself he was telling her all about Eva and Barcelona, even though nothing really happened. Eva was actually completely annoying—all she wanted to talk about was reality TV and Justin Timberlake, and when she finally leaned over at a tapas bar at two A.M. over toast points spread with chocolate and fleur de sel, and suggested that they go back to her place to drink some wine, he was totally over it. But, just looking at Madison, he completely lost his cool. He *wanted* her to think that he'd spent the whole trip fighting off Euro-hotness like it was his full-time summer job. As she sat there, so distant and unflappable, he couldn't help wondering if she'd really even missed him at all.

And it pissed him off.

As he sat there watching Madison pretend to drink her latte, he couldn't help but get the sinking sensation that she no longer cared. She hadn't written to him all summer—despite the fact that he hung out in Internet cafés checking his e-mail at least three times a week. And her silence fueled his silence until he was too scared to be the one to e-mail first—though an annoying little voice told him that he probably should have.

Drew watched as a guy at the table next to him leaned over and brushed his girlfriend's dark hair behind one small, shell-like ear, his hand lingering for a moment on the smooth skin of her neck. *Oh shit.* Maybe he wasn't the only one flirting in cafés all summer long. Madison was gorgeous, desirable, and—most important—available. It was entirely possible—no, probable—that there was someone else already. The thought made him want to dump boiling coffee all over himself and start screaming uncontrollably.

The waitress came back just then, setting his check down on the table and turning away, her hip accidentally knocking Drew's shoulder, spilling his now lukewarm coffee over his clenched hand. "I'm so sorry," the waitress said, offering Drew the stack of paper towels she had tucked away in her apron.

"Don't worry about it," Drew said brusquely, immensely irritated by the spill, by the fact that the coffee didn't burn, by the fact that he wanted it to burn in the first place. He picked up the five-dollar bill Mad had left behind and slid it in his pocket. What was it exactly that Madison was doing to his mind? He needed to get a handle on himself. While he had never had a problem with feeling slightly controlled sexually by Madison's enticing exercises in style that *just* covered this or showed *almost* too much of that, he was less than entertained that his lust had led to this current predicament.

Maybe it's time to move on, to give up, he thought dejectedly while paying the check (skipping over the euros this time) and walking to the door.

Stepping out onto the street, he caught the eye of a plain but pretty girl as she stepped into the café, her pale red hair swinging around her heart-shaped face, a dusting of freckles strewn across her small nose like grains of nutmeg. She smiled at him as he held the door open for her, and when her gray eyes met his, he felt his heart rush. Ah, the thrill of flirting . . . how long had it been since he'd felt that way with Mad? Probably since the seconds before he popped the cork of that bottle of Dom in the park. But whether it had been his fault or not, he knew it was time for something new. The red-haired girl's open smile flashed through his mind as he walked up the street toward home, and he found himself thinking of that new girl, Casey— she had the same cute spray of freckles across her cheeks . . .

Wasn't she as not-Madison as anyone could possibly get? And wasn't that *exactly* what he needed?

you'd better shop around . . .

"Oh my God!" Phoebe Reynaud squealed, holding up a Stella McCartney sundress in crisp white cotton with a splashy red hibiscus print. "I'm *so* buying this tout de suite!"

"It's the hotness," Sophie conferred, her blond head disappearing into a Ralph Lauren argyle sweater in luscious shades of turquoise and green. She pulled the soft wool down across the bright orange Marni dress she was currently wearing, and flounced over to the full-length mirror, her yellow Tory Burch flats slapping against the slickly polished floor. "Ugh," she said, rolling her eyes and pulling the sweater back over her head, her hair crackling with static, "I look like a retarded librarian in this!"

"Oh *right*," Phoebe snorted. "Like you even know where

the library *is*." Phoebe threw the Stella dress over one arm like it was a bag of potato chips, and began sorting through a bin of cashmere sweaters in lime green and burnt orange.

"True." Sophie giggled, sucking at her cinnamon streusel iced latte and leaning into the mirror, sweeping her long bangs to the side with one hand while she inspected the metallic silver Too Faced liner streaked across her top lids. "But why go to the library when the Internet is *so* much more convenient?"

Casey held on to the venti Colombian iced coffee she'd bought at Starbucks before entering the Inner Sanctum otherwise known as Barneys, and pretended to flip through the racks stuffed with designer merchandise she'd only read about in the issues of *In Style* magazine delivered every month to her doorstep back in Normal: Nanette Lepore, Marc Jacobs, Prada, Dolce & Gabbana, and Versace.

Casey had to admit—being in a place like this made her kind of hate shopping—it was all about what she *couldn't* have. As she stood there pretending to seriously consider a Free People beaded tunic in burnt sienna, Casey wondered how long she could stand *not* looking at the price tags. She was terrified that if all those extra zeros actually registered in her caffeine-addled brain, she'd sink into a clothing-induced coma like some twenty-first-century Sleeping Beauty—except that instead of snoozing away peacefully in a glass coffin, she'd be buried under a pile of Ana Molinari kimonos. As if she wasn't feeling intimidated *enough* at the present moment. Looking around at the minimalist décor (nothing to detract from the clothes s'il vous plait), and pricey garments hanging everywhere,

Casey felt more like a bull in a china shop than ever around the acres of expensive, silky fabric.

Casey sighed, fingering a pair of buttery-soft Ralph Lauren leather pants in the perfect fall shade of burnt leaves. She hadn't even worked up the courage to try anything on yet—not that Phoebe and Sophie had noticed. They were too busy walking back and forth, their arms loaded with skimpy silk dresses, flirty lace blouses, and sleek tweed pants, piling what seemed like the whole store in one of the huge, brightly lit dressing rooms like they did this every day of the week. And to be honest, they probably did. Casey couldn't help but think about Marissa and Brandy as she watched Phoebe and Sophie horde clothes like there was an imminent nuclear attack on its way. If her friends back home were there with her, it would've been a totally different experience. They'd be clowning around, trying on clothes they knew none of them could afford—then throwing everything back on the crowded racks and walking into the mall to get ice cream, or browse in Best Buy for new CDs. Everyone would've left the mall equals, because they'd all be in the same, broke boat. As Phoebe's and Sophie's pile of clothing grew larger still, Casey began to worry about the moment they'd approach the register, the moment when Phoebe and Sophie would realize that she wasn't really planning to buy anything at all, that she couldn't afford to. Then they'd look at her with undisguised loathing—or pity. Casey wasn't sure what was worse.

"Oh my God," Sophie yelled out, holding a pair of black Dior hot pants up to her tiny torso. "I have so many pairs of these shorts—it's like a fucking disease with me!" Phoebe giggled from the depths of a white cashmere sweater she was pulling over her head. "I'm trying them on anyway," Sophie said decisively, throwing the shorts over her arm.

There was no way Casey was trying anything on—that was for sure. Not only was it pointless, since she *really* couldn't afford to buy anything, but she'd probably wind up ripping a Missoni sweater as she pulled it over her enormous head, and that the salesgirls, wherever they were hiding, would beat her with old issues of *Vogue* until she surrendered her credit card, which her mother had given her in case of emergencies *only*. Pulling a ruffled Theory sundress in ocean blues and greens from the overstuffed rack, Casey wondered if a back-to-school outfit might be just the kind of emergency her mother was referring to . . .

Sophie's phone began to beep nosily from the depths of her Marc by Marc Jacobs cream leather tote. She dug it out distractedly and surveyed the waiting text message. "Its Mad," she said, dropping the pile of Ralph Lauren plaid skirts she was currently holding to the floor in a heap of tartan. "She's coming to meet us."

Casey's stomach immediately dropped to her beat-up green Pumas. Perfect. Ever since that scene in the park yesterday, Casey had been dreading this moment. Madison made Casey feel like a second-grader with chocolate-pudding-stained hands, or like she had a giant booger hanging out of her nose at all times. And what was she going to say anyway—nice dress, but I think I like your boyfriend? Yeah, *that* would undoubtedly go over stunningly—like everything else that came out of her mouth lately. Casey looked down at the American Eagle dirty-wash capris and the plain white tank she'd bought at the mall before she'd left the Midwest, and wondered how long it would take Madison to say something less than supportive about her disaster of a wardrobe. Well, it could've been worse—at least she wasn't wearing Abercrombie again . . .

When Madison walked in, giant blue-tinted Betsey Johnson shades covering her eyes, the sweet rosy scent of Marc Jacobs Blush perfume trailing in her wake, Casey wanted to run and hide under the tall racks of clothes the way she did when she was four and her mother would drag her shopping. But somehow Casey knew that diving under a pile of Diane von Furstenberg wrap dresses wouldn't exactly solve her problems. If she was ever going to break through the thick ice surrounding the impenetrable Madison Macallister, she was going to have to suck it up and face her new frenemy—head on.

"What up?" Mad intoned with as much excitement as the computer in 2001, air-kissing both Sophie and Phoebe so as not to risk smudging the shiny pink DuWop gloss coating her lips. "How's the makeover going?" Madison stared at Casey from over her shades with a sweeping glance that registered everything from Casey's out-of-control curly head, to her dirty-sneakered feet. "Or haven't you *started* yet?"

Casey noticed that even though Madison's voice dripped sarcasm, as usual, that she immediately started biting her bottom lip while flipping through racks of clothes, the hangers clanging against each other with every angry flick of her obviously practiced wrist. Was she still mad about yesterday? Did she want to shove a hanger in Casey's eye, blinding her instantly so she could no longer moon over her not-really-maybe-sort of boyfriend anymore? Whatever the case, it was obvious to Casey that this girl had mastered the art of being pissy. In fact, Casey thought, watching Madison survey a printed halter top, then flick past it, shuddering lightly, she could probably offer a master course on bitchy clothes-flinging at the New School—Diva Dressing 101.

"How about this?" Sophie said, holding up a Nile green linen sheath dress. "With flat gold sandals, I think it would rock."

"Uh, yeah—if she were going to Tavern on the Green with her fucking *parents*, maybe," Madison snapped, pulling the dress from Sophie's hands and shoving it back on the rack. "Not Meadowlark on her first day of *junior year*." Sophie shrugged her shoulders daintily, shooting Casey a smile that said, "She can't help being such a bitch—but we kind of love her anyway."

Better you than me, Casey thought, as Phoebe ran over with a pair of Paper Denim and Cloth jeans, and a white Imitation of Christ tank embellished with rhinestones.

"I've got it," Phoebe purred, setting the clothes on the rack directly in front of Madison and smoothing her sleek, dark ponytail with one hand.

"Got what?" Madison said, cackling, running one hand over the super-soft cotton of the tank. "Dementia? She's not going gallery hopping in Chelsea for fuck's sake!" Madison tossed the jeans to the floor and prepared to do the same with the tank. "Hang on a minute," she said, holding the shirt up to her chest and walking over to the full-length mirror. "This wouldn't be half bad on me, actually," Madison mused, turning from the left to the right, and examining her predictably perfect self in the long sheet of reflective glass.

"But I haven't accessorized yet!" Phoebe whined, picking the jeans up and placing them back on the rack. "I thought with some chunky silver jewelry and chrome aviators, maybe?"

"There's no accessorizing your way out of this one," Madison drawled, throwing the sparkly tank on top of her Fendi bag she had tossed on the floor like a used Kleenex. "It's entirely the wrong message." Casey watched speechless as Madison marched over to the sale rack, her sandals clacking decisively. "Now this," she said, her voice radiating satisfaction, "is what we call perfection." In her hands Madison held a pale yellow, off-the-shoulder Nanette Lepore sundress, shot through with the faintest lines of metallic gold thread, an understated ruffle decorating the knee-length hem. "With some cute wedge sandals," Madison said, walking over to Casey and holding the dress up to her shoulders, "it will be *beyond* cuteness." Madison looked into Casey's gray eyes and smiled, but since she was still wearing those enormous shades, Casey couldn't quite tell whether Madison was laughing with her— or *at* her.

"Maybe I'll try it on," Casey mumbled, surreptitiously fingering the price tag, her face turning white as she flipped it over, peering at the numbers scribbled in red pen. $350? On sale? Casey felt dizzily nauseous—like she might at any moment go completely Exorcist and projectile vomit green slime all over Madison's perfect coral pedicure. "Umm, I don't know," Casey said weakly, hanging the dress on the nearest rack before she fainted. "I'm not sure it's really me after all."

"What are you *talking* about?" Madison said, grabbing the dress off the rack and pushing it back into Casey's hands. "Of course it's you! It couldn't be *more* you—and to be honest, it's a *hell* of a lot better than what you have on right now." Casey wished the floor would simply open up and swallow her whole—along with everything in the store she didn't have the money to pay for.

"It really is to die for, Casey," Sophie said, fingering the smooth cotton. "You'll be completely adorabubble!" she squealed loudly, grabbing Casey's hand in her own and flinging her bangs from her eye with a practiced toss of her head. "Drew won't be able to keep his eyes *off* you!"

"Oy." Phoebe rubbed her ear with one hand. "No more lattes for you." she said grumpily. "I think you broke my eardrum."

"Come on, Casey." Madison's voice was honey-sweet. "Go try it on—we'll wait here."

Casey could feel herself beginning to sweat. She could feel it rolling down her sides and into the denim of her capris. Gross. How was she going to get out of this one? Maybe she could buy the dress and return it later—except she didn't know if the limit on her mom's credit card even went up that high, and how would she explain to Madison why she wasn't wearing the dress tomorrow at school? No, the only thing she could do was to tell the truth—and if they thought she was a loser and dumped her outside on the steaming pavement of Madison Avenue, so be it.

"Actually, guys," she said, staring at the floor, "I kind of blew my whole allowance last week getting ready to move here." Casey could feel her cheeks getting redder and redder—her whole face felt like she'd dipped it in gasoline and lit a match. She could feel her palms sweating all over the soft yellow dress in her hands, and she took a deep breath. "So I'll just have to make do with what I have for a while."

OK, so it wasn't exactly the truth—but she was going to look stupid enough as it was. There was no sense informing The Bram Clan that she'd probably *never* have the kind of money necessary to shop at Barneys, was there? Hadn't they figured it out already? She was a clueless loser from ass-crack Illinois, who didn't know a Manolo from a Mint Milano, and what's worse, before this totally humiliating moment, she'd half-convinced herself that she was actually fitting in with the most popular girls in school—hell, on the entire Upper East Side, or on the *planet*, for all she knew. Now, all she wanted to do was go back to Nanna's apartment and eat a pint of Häagen-Dazs chocolate-chocolate chip straight from the carton until her brain was totally numb.

Casey looked up, watching as Madison slid her shades off, her green eyes softening as she took in Casey's flushed, embarrassed face. Casey noticed that Madison's eye makeup was smudged—almost as if she'd been crying. But what the hell could Madison Macallister ever have to cry about? Casey couldn't begin to imagine, but she hoped against hope that some day she might just find out.

"Don't worry about it." Madison took the dress from Casey's hands brusquely, all business now, and proceeded to the register. "That's what Amex is for," she called over her shoulder.

"Or mommy and daddy," Sophie trilled, shoving Phoebe in the ribs.

"Or boyfriends," Phoebe added slyly, pulling her white Chloé sunglasses off her head and down over her dark eyes.

When Madison put the large black Barneys shopping bag into Casey's hands, she felt like throwing her arms around the aloof, groomed-within-an-inch-of-her-life, Upper East Side princess she'd only just met, and giving her a giant hug. So, before she could think too much about it, she did just that.

Maybe we're going to be friends after all! Casey thought with no small amount of glee as she leaned in and grabbed Madison, wrapping her freckled arms around Madison's slender frame. "Thanks so much!" Casey gushed, squeezing Madison's alarmingly bony back. "This is so amazing of you!"

Maybe we'll even become best friends, Casey thought, lost in her own happiness and the smell of Madison's Marc Jacobs perfume. *Some random guy definitely wasn't worth causing so much chaos—and shouldn't girls stick together anyway?* After all, the last thing she wanted to do was piss Madison off again, especially after she'd just been so nice to her for absolutely no reason she could think of.

Casey was so lost in her own thoughts that she failed to

realize that Madison wasn't exactly hugging her back until she pulled away. When she stepped back, Madison's face was frozen into a polite smile. *Whoops.* Casey's face fell slightly, and her grip on her shopping bag tightened, her knuckles turning white. *Maybe befriending the most popular girl in school wasn't going to be that easy after all . . .*

games
people
play

Phoebe Reynaud sat smack in the middle of the enormous white shag rug covering the bleached oak wood of her
bedroom floor, trying *not* to listen to the sound of her parents
arguing. You'd think in an apartment the size of a football field
the sound of raised voices wouldn't be a problem—but you'd
be wrong. *You could probably hear them arguing all the way in
Paris*, Phoebe thought, turning up the volume on her iPod
dock to help block out the shouting, filling the custom-
designed, oval-shaped room with the soothing sounds of the
new Feist CD instead. She wished she were back in Paris—the
perfect place for someone like Phoebe, who not only wor-
shipped fashion, but who also aspired to create it someday.
She'd spent the month of June at her grandmother's apartment

just off the Rue Saint-Honoré, popping into Colette and Dior to try on jewel-toned velvet miniskirts and pairs of gorgeous Swarovski crystal–encrusted stilettos, or sitting at a sidewalk café with her sketch pad, drinking Perrier with lemon. If she could've even remotely concentrated with all the screaming and yelling going on around her, Phoebe would've grabbed her pad and drew the silk shantung blouse that had been haunting her since she woke up this morning, and that proceeded to linger at the back of her mind all day. Instead she was curled up on her floor in a ball, trying not to listen to the way her dad was hurling insults at her mother in his own bizarre blend of Franglish.

Tu ne comprends pas la situation! You're nothing more than a common slut! Rien!

She couldn't hear exactly what her mother screamed in return—but her accent was flawless. Even thought she'd spent at least a month of every summer since she was eight in Paris, Phoebe's French skills were still rudimentary at best. Phoebe had no aptitude for languages whatsoever, and she tended to panic when someone asked her even the simplest question— much to her mother's complete dismay. Her menu French was very good: She could order just about anything at a bistro or café with no problem, but her conversational French had always been lousy, no matter how hard she studied. Of course, this was in sharp contrast to her mother, who, despite a childhood spent mainly in New Haven, Connecticut, spoke fluent French—along with Italian, Spanish, *and* German.

"What in the world is *wrong* with you?" Madeline Reynaud

was fond of yelling, usually before she stepped out of the room in a huff, shaking her perfectly coifed satin hair from side to side. "If I had any sense at all, I'd pull you out of Meadowlark and enroll you in the Lycée Français, where you belong!" The Lycée Français was an exclusive private school on East Seventy-fifth Street, where the students were forced to wear stupid, itchy uniforms, and all classes were taught exclusively in French. Phoebe thought it sounded like a French-fried nightmare.

Phoebe wasn't sure how or why it happened, but when she turned thirteen, and people began to notice that she was sort of pretty, her mother started acting like Phoebe was the biggest disappointment of her life—and when she was being honest with herself, Phoebe suspected that it just might be true. Her mother just couldn't stand sharing the spotlight—she needed male attention the way alcoholics needed vodka—and she'd mastered the art of throwing a star-fit whenever anyone dared compliment Phoebe on how lovely she was. Phoebe had begun to dread those moments, watching as her mother's surgically tightened skin froze like a mask, her eyes glazing over with annoyance.

Madeline Ashbrook had arrived on the Manhattan debutante circuit a fresh, rosy girl of eighteen with jet-black hair and flashing Caribbean-blue eyes that bewitched any man within fifty yards, including Phoebe's father, Etienne Reynaud, who'd moved to the United State at seventeen to attend Harvard. But now, with forty rapidly approaching, and her father's attention decidedly waning, Phoebe often found her mother staring into mirrors for hours at a time, pulling back the skin of her jaw or eyelids while muttering under her breath. She was still earth-shatteringly gorgeous—for a woman of a certain age. But the cosmetic procedures she was forever subjecting herself to weren't helping any. All the Botox and laser resurfacing she spent thousands on only made her look more like an alien, and not a particularly youthful alien either.

Phoebe heard the tinny, contagious sound of giggling coming from her sister's room across the hall, and she got up and cautiously opened her bedroom door. The sound of breaking glass against the imported Italian tiles in her parents' bathroom drowned out her sister's laughter, and made Phoebe jump out of her room and out onto the slick, polished floors of the hallway. Phoebe knocked lightly on the large pink metallic star Bijoux had pasted to her bedroom door. "Beebs? You in there?" She swung it open.

Bijoux sat behind a reproduction of a Chippendale desk—perfect in every detail—except that it was scaled to the size of a six-year-old's body. Even though the maid had probably picked her up hours ago, Bijoux was still wearing the pink tutu and dirty white leotard she'd worn to ballet class earlier that afternoon, and a pair of their mother's black Chanel reading glasses sat on the bridge of her tiny nose, magnifying her blue eyes, making them look gigantic. Her room was painted a shiny, candy pink, and an Austrian-crystal chandelier hung over her flouncy, pink-and-white ruffled bed. Her best friend, Jeremy Alexander, sat across from the desk wearing jeans and a red Abercrombie T-shirt with pictures of monster trucks on it.

They were both sucking on Bomb Pops, their mouths stained with the red and blue dye.

"Now," Bijoux said, peering over the glasses and trying to sit up straight in her chair, "you *did* sign a pre-nup, didn't you?"

Jeremy giggled, squirming around on his miniature Chippendale chair, and when he opened his mouth Phoebe could see that his tongue was bright blue. "No," he said, grinning at Phoebe, who was still standing in the doorway, one hand on her hip, "I don't think so."

"What are you little monsters up to?" Phoebe smiled, walking over to her sister and kissing her on the top of her dark ponytailed head, breathing in the sweet scent of baby shampoo along with Givenchy's signature perfume for the under-seven set, Tartine et Chocolat.

"We're just playing, Pheebs," Bijoux said as she placed her rapidly melting Bomb Pop down on the desk, grabbed a magic wand covered with silver glitter off the floor, and promptly began waving it in her sister's face.

Phoebe grabbed the wand, halting it in midair. "Playing *what?*"

"Divorce court," Jeremy said matter-of-factly, bending down to grab Bijoux's ankle under the desk.

"Eeeeeeeeeeeeeeeeeee," Bijoux screamed, yanking her ankle away from Jeremy and tearing around the room like someone had just put a live tarantula in her tutu. Even though Bijoux could be a holy terror, everyone loved her—the doormen, taxi drivers, puppies, strangers on the street—and, of course she was Mommy's little darling as well. Madeline was constantly cooing over her youngest daughter, dressing Bijoux in bizarre high-fashion outfits like she was a real-life American Girl doll. All this should've made Phoebe positively despise her baby sister—and the attention she routinely got from their mother—but strangely, it didn't. Bijoux was the person Phoebe loved most in the world, and the only one she really trusted.

Phoebe grabbed her sister by the waist and sat down on the round pink rug on the floor, pulling Bijoux down onto her lap and grabbing a juice-stained Harry Potter book from the corner of the desk. "Maybe if you little maniacs can sit still for five minutes," Phoebe said into Bijoux's ear, "I'll read to you guys for a while—unless you'd rather keep playing."

"We'll play later," Bijoux said bossily, pulling the book from Phoebe's hands and opening it to the beginning. "It's an open-and-shut case of sexual abandonment." Bijoux reached up and smacked her sister on the forehead with her small, open palm, smiling mischievously. "Now, *reeeeead*, Pheebs!"

Bratlet, Phoebe thought affectionately as Jeremy snuggled up next to her on the floor, and she began to read. Bijoux stuck her thumb in her mouth the way she always did when she was being read to, sucking softly and breathing loudly through her nose as Phoebe turned the pages. It was ridiculous—her little sister was playing divorce court and before long her parents would probably be *visiting* divorce court—it practically defined the word *ironic*. Even though she barely saw her father as it was, Phoebe knew that if her parents split up for good, her mother's moods would only get worse, and Phoebe really didn't know if she'd be able to handle it.

Please don't let them get divorced, Phoebe thought as the thick paper sliced the pad of her index finger, giving her an excuse to cry. Tears sprang from the corners of her dark, almond-shaped eyes and rolled silently down her cheeks as she struggled to keep her voice steady, and held on to Bijoux for dear life.

it's a
different
world
than where
you come
from . . .

Casey stood nervously in Meadlowlark Academy's shiny chrome and glass Dining Hall, hugging the side of the Whole Bean coffee kiosk like an infinitely shorter, curly-haired jailbird Paris Hilton. Walking into the Dining Room—with its three-course meals designed by Thomas Keller, Pratesi napkins, stainless steel salad bar, and Whole Bean coffee kiosk—was like stepping onto another planet, one where the aliens used lots of Frederic Fekkai hair products, and overdosed on Frappuccinos and Diet Snapple. And it couldn't have been more different than the peeling, lime-colored cafeteria she'd left behind at Normal High, with its prepackaged mac and cheese, frozen fish sticks, and greasy burgers.

The kiosk, a popular meeting place for caffeine-deprived

students before, after, and sometimes during class, was completely packed, and Casey had to sip her Apple Whipped Caramel iced latte down to a manageable level to avoid spilling the fancypants drink all over her spanking-new yellow sundress. Usually, she hated stupidly overpriced, high-end coffee, but as soon as she put her new clothes on this morning, she'd been fighting the slightly creepy feeling that she'd become someone else entirely. Someone who spent three hours in the bathroom getting ready for school, only to then show up and order the most preposterously complicated java on the menu. And her new dress, and Jimmy Choo cork wedge heels borrowed from Sophie's endless closet, only made her feel even more out of place and less like herself—whoever *that* was anymore.

Casey tried to breathe steadily, but with the amount of caffeine rushing through her sleep-deprived system, it was hard to keep her pulse from racing or her palms from sweating around the plastic cup. Ugh—she was the only person she knew whose hands could sweat while holding an ice-filled cup. She'd sat up for hours the night before, giddy with anticipation and fear, gripping her violin with white-knuckled fingers and practicing scales with frenzied intensity, until Nanna's crackly, sleepy voice yelled through the wall for her to "cut the crap and go to sleep already." As she lay in bed, staring across her cluttered room at her new dress hanging on the back of the door, she couldn't help imagining what she'd say to Drew when she saw him today—and what he might say back. *So much for girls sticking together*, she thought, licking whipped cream from the rim of her cup. *I guess lust is definitely stronger than friendship*. Not that you could really call them friends anyway. The thought made Casey kind of sad. She hadn't known how much she missed having real friends until she'd moved away and lost them.

Even though Madison's offer to buy Casey the dress definitely crossed the line from acquaintance to something more personal, Casey wasn't sure if she'd ever get close enough to Madison to really consider her a real friend—whatever that meant. Casey had never met anyone truly rich before now, but she did know—mostly from watching shows like *Laguna Beach and The Hills* on MTV—that people with money lived in a different world, maybe even a different universe. And standing there in a ridiculously expensive dress she didn't pay for, for the first time Casey wondered if she'd been bought along with it, and she didn't like the way it made her stomach suddenly queasy, despite the mouth-watering aromas of fresh croissants and roasted veggie omelets permeating the room.

In spite of the sudden nausea and the whipped cream–filled coffee—or maybe in protest of it—Casey's stomach started to growl loudly. The girl standing next to her, wearing a pair of heavily distressed Seven jeans and the same Imitation of Christ tank Madison bought yesterday, paused while sending an e-mail on her BlackBerry to give Casey a disgusted look.

"There's, like, *food* over there, you know," she said, staring at Casey from behind an oversize pair of pink-lensed Gucci aviators. "Breakfast? You've heard of it? The most important meal of the day?" Casey opened her mouth, then closed it again, unsure of how to respond. The girl's hair was straightened within an inch of its life, and it stopped at her exposed collarbones in a razor-sharp bob. "Or, there's always the rexie table," she said, pointing at a large table farthest away from the food, filled with a group of extraordinarily pale, wan-looking girls whose collective body weight probably equaled *one* of the Olsen twins. The rexies were bent over their textbooks, their nutrient-deficient locks hanging limply around pinched faces. A single, cut-up apple sat on a napkin in the center of the table, and not one of the girls acknowledged—much less ingested— the rapidly browning slices. "They're on the Kleenex diet."

Kleenex diet? That couldn't be what it sounded like, could it?

"They eat Kleenex instead of food," scarily hip-girl said in a tone that insinuated that Casey was quite possibly the stupid- est life form on planet earth. "Models do it to get ready before Fashion Week," she went on, as if that explained everything.

"I'm not . . ." Casey said, stammering. "I mean, I *eat*."

The girl lowered her aviators, exposing expertly applied black shadow flecked with silver glitter. "Sure you do," she said, her voice a flat monotone. She gave Casey one final look up and down before walking away, already engrossed in a conversation on her wireless headset just as Drew Van Allen walked through the doorway.

Casey's heart began to race and all at once she realized she was totally panicking. She wanted to run out of the Dining Hall and never come back—or throw herself in his arms and declare her undying lust. Why was talking to guys so com- pletely stressful? Casey pulled her already out-of-control curls behind her ears and tried to look contemplative as she studied her apple latte like it held the riddle of the Sphinx.

Drew shuffled over to the register, sunglasses on, and ordered a coffee. In his Triple Five Soul cargos and white button-down shirt, his tanned arms protruded from the rolled-up sleeves, he was even cuter than she remembered. In fact, he was perfect. Would he even remember her? And, more importantly, would he even talk to her? Casey's thoughts raced as fast as the caffeine rushing through her veins. *Crap. Why do I have to sweat so much all the time? Is my hair frizzing yet? Why am I such a moron?*

Casey smoothed down the polished cotton of her skirt as Drew removes his shades, taking a long, greedy gulp of coffee as he looked up, his gaze meeting hers. Drew's face looked totally blank—and the black sunglasses didn't help. *Oh God, he doesn't even remember me!* Casey thought with no small amount of dismay, her stomach flipping over as she shifted her weight from her left foot to her right. *And these stupid shoes are killing me.*

"Hi," Casey mouthed, scraping up every ounce of courage she possessed, then looked away. If he didn't come over, she was probably going to pass out or die of embarrassment right on the spot, holding her stupid froufrou coffee drink, which she didn't really want anyway. They could just throw some roasted veggies and organic tater tots on top of her and bury her right there, and Madison and the rest of Meadowlark would surely walk on top of her in their ankle-snapping stiletto sandals, completely oblivious to her prostrate corpse.

"Hey, beautiful." Casey heart jumped as she looked up into Drew's grinning face. He'd even shaved for the first day back, and the skin of his throat looked so soft that she had to dig her fingernails into her palm to keep from touching it. "You look really . . ." Drew gestured with one hand at the length of her body, taking in the dress and shoes as he bent his tousled dark head and sipped at his coffee, "different." Drew pulled off his shades and slid them into his bright blue Timbuk2 messenger bag.

"Yeah . . ." Casey said sarcastically, her voice way more confident than she actually felt. "I'm wearing a *dress*."

"I can see that," Drew said, his lips curving into a smirk, his eyes giving her an appreciative once-over. "But, why are you standing here all by yourself?" Drew grinned, obviously enjoying their bantering. "Did you scare away all your potential suitors?"

"Yeah, right," Casey scoffed, blushing even harder and mentally ordering her face to return to its normal freckly paleness. Madison would know exactly how to get her flirt on—but then again she wasn't Madison, not by a long shot. Realistically, at this point in the conversation, Madison would probably have Drew buying her lattes, promising to do her laundry, and eating dry cereal out of the palm of her hand.

"So," Drew said, toying with the lid of his coffee, still flashing his bright-white smile, which was starting to make Casey feel even more uncomfortable.

"So yeah," Casey replied, feeling as if there was a giant red neon sign floating over both of their heads, the tall angular letters flashing AWKWARD SILENCE in a red light bright enough to cast a sheen on the rexies across the room that would make them pass for living beings.

Say something saysomething saysomethingsaysomething!

"So . . . being new pretty much sucks, huh?" Drew said, a wry grin on his deliciously apple-red lips. "And I should know—I transferred in the middle of freshman year. Before that, we lived all the way downtown."

"Really?" Casey said, her heart leaping, It was more than she dared hope for. He was new, she was new—clearly it was meant to be. It was kismet—right in the middle of a cafeteria that smelled enticingly of freshly brewed lattes and cinnamon rolls. "Wow, it seems like you've been here forever."

"It definitely *feels* like forever sometimes," Drew said sarcastically.

"So maybe there's still hope for me yet . . ." Casey smiled, wishing she could stop sweating for even five minutes.

"A few weeks will pass and you won't even feel new anymore," Drew said reassuringly, his blue eyes so bright and clear that Casey had to force herself to look away just so she wouldn't become hypnotized. "And by the way, I'm having this party a week from this Saturday. Well, *I'm* not really having it, my parents are. But it's for me." Drew coughed and looked away. "It'll probably be totally lame, but you should come anyway."

Casey tried to smile and looked at her scarily unpainted toes. It wasn't exactly the most convincing invitation she'd ever heard. "OK," she said nodding, "maybe I will."

"So," Drew said, gulping the last of his coffee and throwing the plastic cup in the trash, "can I get your digits? I still owe you a private tour."

"That's true," Casey said, her heart beating so fast she thought it might explode out of her chest and splatter all over the creamy beige walls of the Dining Hall.

"But anybody can show you around Meadowlark," Drew said, grinning widely, "I was thinking of something a little more . . . interesting."

Oh my God, he's actually asking me out on a date! Casey tried her best to look nonchalant, but like a scene out of a bad teen comedy, the hand clutching her coffee starting shaking wildly, making her nervousness completely transparent. She didn't have a ton of experience flirting with guys, and she wondered abstractly if she was even doing it right. Was there a formula? Maybe she could find some sort of chart on the Internet . . .

Drew looked down at her cup, a quizzical look on his face.

"Too much coffee," Casey blurted out, tossing the cup in the trash.

"Clearly." Drew smiled, pushing a shock of thick hair from his forehead. "So," he said, taking a deep breath before continuing, "how about a private tour of the city? I promise to share all the secret hot spots and insider info. You in?"

"I'm in," Casey said, smiling into his dark blue eyes, feeling that if her stomach dropped any more toward her shoes, she'd have to send out a search party to eventually locate it. "Definitely."

"Cool." Drew pulled his cell from the pocket of his cargos and flipped it open. "Give me your number and I'll call you later."

Casey couldn't believe it, she felt like she'd just won the

New York Lottery. Drew Van Allen had not only just asked her out, but now her number was, even as they spoke, being programmed into his cell phone—where hopefully it would stay for all eternity! This was it: It had to be love.

"It's three-oh-nine—"

Drew's fingers halted on the keypad, and his eyes moved as if transfixed to the doorway. Casey broke off, her number incomplete as Drew continued to stare over her shoulder like he'd become suddenly hypnotized, a strange look coming over his face. "Uh, let's pick this up later," he mumbled, shooting her a weak smile and putting his shades back on before turning around and walking quickly away.

Casey stood there watching as the rexies gathered up their apple slices, throwing them in the trash. What had she done? Was she being too forward? Did her hair get frizzy? Or worse yet, did he suddenly realize just how uncool she really was? Casey's face fell dejectedly, as she turned around to see Madison standing in the doorway, flanked by Phoebe and Sophie.

Madison wore a silky, lime green, peasant-style dress, the spaghetti straps accentuating her burnished tan, her hair falling to her shoulders in a wave of silken strands. Suddenly, Casey felt like she was wearing an old dishrag and some dental floss. Madison's A-line skirt only served to make her already long legs look impossibly gazelle-like, and her skin was clear and golden, her lips brushed with just the faintest touch of rosy gloss. She was, in every way, the definition of teenage perfection. Casey sighed dejectedly. She might as well tie a cement block to her feet and throw herself in the Hudson River. How was she ever going to compete with someone as jaw-droppingly gorgeous as Madison Macallister when she was just . . . a normal *girl*—and one who didn't even know how to give herself a pedicure at that.

Casey watched with something not unlike the fear the rexies experienced daily when confronting even the tiniest morsel of food as Drew paused briefly at Madison's side as she half-turned her body to greet him. Even though Casey couldn't hope to hear what they were saying, Madison's stance—her very presence—spoke volumes. She was sexy without even trying: The way she simply stood there dared the entire male population *not* to rip her clothes off on the spot. Casey drew in a sharp breath when she noticed that even though Madison's attention appeared to be solely on Drew, her cat-eyed gaze was focused directly on Casey, the faintest tinge of a smile moving over Madison's glossy lips.

Please let him turn around and smile—or at least wave, Casey pleaded silently, unable to tear her eyes away from the sight of Madison and Drew together in the halls of Meadowlark once again, a place they both clearly belonged. Watching them together, it was clear to Casey that they belonged not only in this world, but to each other as well. Casey looked at her shoes, her vision blurring. She couldn't compete with Madison Macallister. No one could.

And as Casey looked up to watch Drew walk out of the Dining Hall without turning around, Casey thought of her number in Drew's cell, incomplete—like their conversation.

And she knew that even if every last digit of her number *did* someday make it all the way into Drew's phone that, alphabetically speaking, Macallister would still *always* come before McCloy . . .

little
white
lies

⊕

As Madison entered the Dining Hall, her eyes locked upon the heinous sight of Drew wrapped in an intense-looking convo with Casey. Until that moment, the day had been aces. She'd woken up before the alarm went off, which for her was a massive miracle, and after she got out of the shower, totally invigorated from the grainy, citrusy goodness of her Bliss Body Polish, she could just *sense* that it was going to be a good hair day. It was an almost mystical feeling—and as close to spirituality as Madison ever got. When she communed with the hair gods, she couldn't help feeling all glowy and lit up inside—and the feeling just kept getting better as she slid into her new Tadashi pleated chiffon halter dress in the most luscious shade of green . . .

After two double espressos and a short ride in the black Lincoln Town Car that drove her through the urban maze of the same six blocks each morning, she felt totally ready to dominate Meadlowlark, and Drew, for the third straight year. Yesterday was obviously just a blip on the otherwise perfect radar screen of her life. But as she watched Drew pull his cell from his pocket and prepare to enter Casey's digits, Madison felt her ego deflate like someone had pricked a hole in her La Perla gel-insert bra. She'd only just dumped him yesterday! Was he really getting another girl's number one short day later, potentially replacing her? And was that even possible?

Apparently. And, worse yet, it was happening right in front of her face.

Whatever, Madison told herself, taking a Guerlain compact from her wicker-and-suede Rafe bag and calmly applying another coat of Nars gloss in Striptease. *If he thinks I actually care who he flirts with, he's sadly mistaken.* But deep down she had to admit that as she watched Casey lean toward her now probably ex-boyfriend, instead of being filled with excited, caffeinated butterflies, Madison's stomach now felt all twisty and strange. As much as she didn't want to, as much as it practically killed her to even think it, she did care—a lot more than she even wanted to admit to herself. Even from where she was standing, it was obvious that Casey and Drew had the It Factor—there was some serious chemistry going on. If the room suddenly went black, there'd probably be a shower of fucking sparks over their heads. Watching Casey giggle and blush, Madison could no longer deny the obvious anymore. Even though he still hadn't apologized, even though he acted like a idiot time and time again, she still wanted him back . . .

Even if it was just so another girl couldn't have him.

And, besides, Madison told herself as she stood in the doorway of the Dining Hall with Sophie and Phoebe, *this isn't about apologies anymore—this is a total declaration of war.*

"Wow, holy hookup, Batman," Sophie said gleefully, watching as Drew smiled at Casey, who, Madison couldn't help noticing, looked, ugh—it was going to pain her to say it—almost pretty in her new dress, even though Sophie's shoes were *so* totally last year. When she arrived at Barneys yesterday she certainly wasn't planning on buying Casey *anything*—it kind of just . . . happened. After walking out on Drew, she was feeling all vulnerable *and* angry—a combination she hated more than anything because it made her feel helpless—and more than anything in the world, Madison needed to feel like everything was under control. Come to think of it, Drew was so infuriating that she had probably been suffering from a fucking case of Post Traumatic Stress. After all, it wasn't like she usually went out of her way to be nice to total strangers. She should've spent the day at Silver Hill getting "occupational therapy" with all the other nutcases, not back-to-school shopping as if she hadn't gone temporarily insane. But, as she stood there watching as Casey fiddled uncomfortably with the price tag, her face getting redder by the second, Madison suddenly felt kind of sorry for her. But now, as she noticed how the daffodil-colored cotton brought out the highlights in Casey's blond curls, Madison wished more than anything that she'd simply ignored the uncomfortable look on Casey's face and put the stupid dress back on the sale rack where it belonged.

So this is what you get for being nice to people, Madison thought sourly. *You get your sort-of boyfriend stolen from right under your nose by some Midwestern moron.* Well, if this was what being nice was all about, she'd rather go back to being a complete bitch. At least then she'd always be in control.

Madison turned to glare at Sophie, who had dressed for the first day of school in her Bohemian Socialite look: a pair of Ralph by Ralph Lauren pink capris, a floaty, ethereal Free People tunic sprigged with tiny embroidered pink and white flowers, and a pair of bright pink YSL wedge sandals on her feet. The whole ensemble (or train wreck, depending who you asked) was topped off with a large, floppy white straw hat that hid most of her face from plain view.

"What?" Sophie asked innocently, a bemused expression sliding over her glowing, spray-tanned features: "What did I say?" Sophie had a habit of pretending she was dumb when it suited her, mostly when she felt like she was about to get in some kind of trouble. And looking at her smooth, open face and blond hair, you'd almost believe it. Unless you were her best friend, and knew that she had gotten a near-perfect score on her last SAT practice test.

Phoebe pulled her black quilted Chanel tote higher on her shoulder and pushed up her Muse shades to get a better look at Casey's outfit. "She does look cute though," Phoebe proclaimed with a decisive nod, straightening the ties on her YaYa silk wrap blouse in a delicate shade of orchid that offset her creamy complexion perfectly, and paired well with her newest pair of dark-washed Citizens of Humanity jeans and gold D&G slides. "But not as cute as me, of course," Phoebe murmured, giving herself the once-over in the long bank of mirrors lining the far wall of the Dining Hall before realizing her obvious faux pas. She turned to Madison in a desperate attempt to save face and smiled sweetly. "Or *you*," she said.

"What about *me*?" Sophie said, and Madison wondered for the trillionth time how somebody could manage to giggle and whine at the same time—Sophie had practically made it an art form.

"What *about* you," Madison snapped, willing Drew to look up and notice her. At that moment, almost as if she'd scripted it, Drew glanced at the doorway, his face draining of color as his blue-eyed gaze came to rest on his oldest friend—or worst enemy at Meadowlark. Madison smiled, lifting one hand to wave as her gold Louis Vuitton charm bracelet slid to her forearm. She couldn't help taking a perverse amount of satisfaction in the way Drew's expression suddenly changed, turning closed off and serious. He snapped his phone shut and walked quickly away from Casey, who stood there in disbelief, mouth open.

Madison's eyes narrowed as Drew approached. There was no way he was going to be able to exit the Dining Hall without passing her, and she was going to love every minute of his impending discomfort.

"Going somewhere?" she purred, raising one perfectly arched blond brow.

"Oui," Drew said brusquely, preparing to brush past her. "French class—sucks to be me."

"In more ways than one," Madison said sarcastically as Drew walked out the door, leaving Sophie and Phoebe exchanging shocked glances. Madison glared at his back, the adrenaline pumping in her veins from their brief encounter. Well, she had all day to get things back where they belonged—with her on top, figuratively speaking . . .

"Well, that redefined the concept of 'a quickie,'" Phoebe said as soon as Drew was out of earshot.

"For real," Sophie echoed. "It was the total *definition* of brief."

Madison sighed, surveying the line that stretched across the room at the Whole Bean kiosk as Casey approached, weaving unsteadily on her wedges, a bewildered expression still lingering on her freckled face.

"Hey, guys," Casey said, nervously shifting her unruly mess of curls off of one shoulder. Had this girl never heard of a flat iron? Or a hairdresser?

"Hey, yourself." Sophie smiled broadly, removing her hat to reveal her honeyed-hair clipped back neatly at the neck with a heavy silver barrette.

"So, were you and the D-man trading fashion tips?" Phoebe grinned wickedly. "Or was there something a little more . . . personal going on?"

"It was nothing much," Casey said, biting her lip and looking at the floor.

Right. As Madison took in Casey's flushed face and slightly guilty expression she wondered why, if the conversation was so meaningless, couldn't Casey seem to look her in the face?

"He just wants to show me around town sometime," Casey said in a rush, unable to keep a happy smile from creeping over her lips. "That's all."

"Oh my God, that's amaaaaaaazing." Sophie squealed like Brad Pitt had just been let loose in the Dining Hall. "When are you going out?"

"And more importantly," Phoebe interrupted, pushing Solyphie aside with a shove of her elbow, "what are you going to *wear*?" Phoebe looked over at Sophie, a smile hovering over her lips.

"AS LITTLE AS POSSIBLE!" they yelled in unison, slapping each other a high-ten.

What the hell was going on with everyone around here? Madison thought grumpily. The day was getting worse by the second. Let's recap: First she'd walked in on the new girl practically hooking up with Drew in front of practically the entire student body, and now her supposed "friends" were actually cheering this madness on? Whatever happened to loyalty? Well, if this girl actually thought she could handle Drew Van Allen, she had another thing coming. *Maybe*, Madison thought, weighing her options, *there's some way I can help her out* . . .

Madison reached over and placed a manicured hand on Casey's arm, squeezing gently. Her expression, she hoped, displayed exactly the right blend of concern and world-weary we're-in-this-togetherness.

"Forget fashion," she said with a roll of her eyes and a smile, her voice hushed and secretive as she pulled Casey out of the Traitor Twins' earshot. "You need some *real* advice—not makeup tips." Madison turned and shot Phoebe and Sophie a deadly glare before continuing. "Now, I know Drew better than anyone, and what he *really* likes is when girls are kind of aggressive." Madison watched closely as Casey nodded, clearly hanging onto her every word. This was so easy that Madison almost began to feel sorry for her.

"He's actually really shy underneath all his dumbass macho bullshit, so you totally have to make the first move. After all," she added mischievously, "I dated him for like, forever, so I should know." Madison giggled warmly, clutching Casey's arm like they'd been best friends—or worst enemies—all their lives.

"Wow," Casey said, looking up at Madison like she'd just succeeded in reinventing the wheel. "Thanks so much!" Casey leaned toward Madison and her voice dropped to an almost-whisper. "I was kind of worried that you might be . . . mad at me or something,"

"Oh please," Madison snorted, rolling her eyes. "Drew and I are the definition of O-V-E-R. Now, here's what you need to do . . ."

As Madison whispered into Casey's ear, she felt almost guilty about her blatant lie—until she remembered that, until Casey came along, *she* was the one Drew was cornering daily in the Dining Hall. Besides, it would be totally embarrassing to lose Drew to some complete nobody from nowhereville—and Madison didn't *do* embarrassed.

She had to somehow make things go back to normal. Her life had suddenly gone all Shakesperean on her—like something out of *Much Ado About Nothing*—except she was no dumb, love-struck maiden. She was going to keep her wits about her. How else could she possibly strategize effectively? It was like that quote she'd learned in seventh grade by that Euphues guy . . . how did that go again?

Oh yes: All's fair in love and war.

the
gentle art
of
conversation

Casey paused in the hallway, just in front of room 12A and attempted to compose herself before walking into French class. It was her first class of the day, and considering how totally stressful her morning had already been, she was going to need all the composure she could muster to fight her way through an hour of academic intensity *in another goddamn language*. Her experience of Meadlowlark so far had left her completely dazed. Not only did the entire student body dress like they were on their way to Bryant Park for the fall collections, but everyone was screamingly smart. She took a deep breath and let it out slowly through her nose, the way her mother had taught her during her whole spiritual phase last year, when she wore hideous, batik-printed caftans, took up Transcendental

Meditation, and talked endlessly about global warming and solar panels. Except when Casey tried to exhale gracefully, she coughed on the lungful of pine-scented air she had sucked in from the immaculately polished hallway, choking slightly, her eyes suddenly wet.

She bent over, coughing and hacking like a maniac until a total stranger whacked her decisively on the back before opening the door. Casey looked up into the face of a tall guy with dark hair that fell into his eyes, so thin the only way to describe him might be calorically challenged, who was dressed from head to toe in standard-issue Emo gear of black tight jeans and a faded gray T-shirt with the words *My Bloody Valentine* on the front outlined in silver. *Great,* Casey thought, smiling and waving thanks limply as he lurched away, *I can't even breathe right.*

She took another breath, this one decidedly more shallow, and walked into class, tentatively taking a seat in the back of the gleaming room—as far away from Emo-backslapping-boy as she could sit. Looking around the room made her feel like she was on acid: The sheen of the glossy, pale oak floors was so bright and vibrant that it practically sang. In fact, she could almost pick up the faintest melody of *La Marseillaise*. The tiered rows of aluminum desks and the huge window seat stuffed with black-and-white op art–printed cushions spoke more of a hip Soho loft than of advanced placement. Was this really high school? As she looked around at the other students who were busily talking and laughing, the girls all inspecting each other's outfits, the guys punching each other randomly in the shoulders like testosterone-crazed lunatics, Casey couldn't help but wish that she'd made it into the same section as Sophie, Phoebe, and Madison.

Casey sat back in her ergonomic chair, inhaling the scent of fresh paint (the classrooms were retouched each August without fail), as Madame LeCombe, a French woman in her mid-thirties who looked like she put on her makeup with a trowel and consumed men instead of food, sauntered over to her desk in a tight, black pencil skirt and sighed heavily before walking over to a supply closet in the back of the room. When she returned, all Casey could see was the brand-new, shining titanium MacBook in her hands, her short crimson fingernails tapping the metal casing. She held the computer out to Casey, one excessively plucked eyebrow raised.

"Voila!" Madame LeCombe said cheerily, pointing out the jack embedded in the desk where Casey could plug in. When Casey opened the laptop, it hummed and whirred like a happy kitten, and Casey felt suddenly worlds away from the battered PC her mom had bought her three years ago—and Normal High, where the students still took notes on arcane substances like paper and tired their hands out writing with ballpoint pens.

"Thanks!" Casey said, unable to keep the surprise from her voice. "Should I just give this back to you at the end of class?" Madame LeCombe blinked at her uncomprehendingly, and the girl sitting in front of Casey wearing an electric-blue Milly sundress and the highest silver wedge sandals she had ever seen giggled nastily. The girl's chin-length blond hair bobbed healthily up and down as she laughed, and Casey felt her face fill with heat.

"Non, non," Madame LeCombe chided, wagging a jeweled finger in Casey's face, *"c'est pour vous!"* Now she was really confused. Did she really just get to keep this monumentally expensive piece of equipment . . . just because she happened to be enrolled at Meadowlark Academy? Was this standard? It certainly looked that way, as every single student in the twenty-seat classroom had the exact same model MacBook opened up on the desk in front of them, and was staring at her like she was a world-class idiot.

"We all get one," said a voice directly behind her. Casey craned her neck around and came face-to-face with Drew—who was grinning widely.

"Oh," Casey said, turning her body so that she could see him more easily, "I didn't know—nobody told me." Twisted around like a pretzel, Casey felt like her diaphragm was doubled up and pushing into her chest cavity. Or was it just the elastic waistband of her underwear cutting into her overfull stomach? Maybe that second blueberry muffin she'd eaten while listening to Madison's advice was a bad idea . . .

"Yeah," Drew said, removing his own laptop from his messenger bag and opening it onto the desk. "Well, get used to it—free laptops are just the beginning." Drew rolled his blue eyes, smiling crookedly while he fussed with his computer. As she looked at him, Madison's words rang out in her ears—*be aggressive*. The truth was, Casey hadn't had that much experience with guys in general, much less with flirting, and she'd never made the first move either. It wasn't that she liked playing hard to get or anything, she just didn't have any experience playing—period. The only guys she'd ever flirted with had always approached her first . . . and she hadn't exactly managed to come off as a femme fatale then either.

"Commencez votre conversationz," Madame LeCombe called out from her perch on the edge of her desk at the front of the room, her legs crossed, kicking one black stilettoed foot in the air. The chatter in the room suddenly reduced to a low hum, and Casey watched her fellow classmates pair up, turning in their seats to practice their French conversation skills with the person seated directly behind them—which, as far as she could tell, meant that she'd be practicing on . . . Drew.

Casey's pulse started racing so fast she was sure she'd probably have a stroke by the time the bell rang. What was she going to *say*? Her mind was a complete and total blank. Not only did she have to figure out a way to be aggressive, but she had to do it in *French*. It wasn't like she was so great at flirting in English in the first place—and English was her mother tongue! To make matters worse, Casey hadn't exactly paid rapt attention during her French classes back in Normal—mostly she'd stared out the window, dreaming of the day when some ridiculously cute guy would make out with her after school in the parking lot, the ultimate campus hookup spot.

Casey smiled at Drew uncertainly as he closed his laptop, leaning forward, his elbows on the desk.

"Voulez-vous parler avec moi?" Drew said with comic exag-

geration, rolling his R's around in his mouth like it was full of jawbreakers, sounding like a demented Pepe Le Peu.

"*Bien sûr!*" Casey answered confidently. As long as they stayed at this kindergartenesque level of conversation, she could probably handle herself—even though talking to Drew in French felt really cheesy, like she should be wearing a beret, chain-smoking Gauloises, and carrying a baguette.

"*Que faites-vous cet après-midi?*"

What was she doing this afternoon? Was he asking because he was just curious and making conversation, or was he actually asking her *out*? Ugh, was there some kind of bizarro rule that made boys so totally mysterious on a daily basis, even in French? *Be aggressive!* her inner Madison screamed out. *Don't just sit there like a schlub!*

However uncomfortable it made her feel, she knew that she had to go for it—before she lost her nerve completely and ran out of the room. Casey leaned forward, feeling like a complete alien from the planet Don't Date Me, and rested her hand on Drew's arm, gently running her fingertips over his smooth skin. "*Quoi que vous faites,*" she answered, her eyes fixed on his face, her cheeks burning like she'd spent the day lying out in the park with no sunscreen.

Oh my God. Did she really just say: "Whatever you're doing?" More important, did she even say it right? Because he was looking at her like she was a total lunatic, then down at his arm, where her hand still rested. Casey grabbed his hand and turned it over so that the palm faced up, and with her favorite red pen, proceeded to write her phone number in large block letters on his skin. *"Telephonez-moi ce soir,"* she whispered in what she hoped was a sexy voice, feeling the sweat break out under her arms like it had been held back by a dam all this time. Drew looked up, his expression uncertain and slightly queasy-looking, and then back down at the series of numbers penned onto his hand. He had asked for her number in the Dining Hall just a half hour ago—did he have too many lattes at breakfast or something? Whatever was going on, he looked totally uncomfortable, and when he pulled away with a weak smile and looked down at his desk, Casey's heart felt like it'd just been drop-kicked from the top of the Chrysler Building.

"S'il vous plaît ouvrez vos livres au chapitre l'un." Madame LeCombe's voice rang out in the classroom, and Casey turned around gratefully, opening her French book to the first chapter and staring down at a picture of a young French couple entwined on a bench at night, the Eiffel Tower sparkling in the distance. Casey stared dejectedly down at the page, acutely aware of Drew's presence directly behind her, and of the way her skin was tingling like so many insects were crawling up and down her arms and legs. Casey looked at the kissing couple in the picture, and wished more than anything that her life might be even half as romantic as that of a couple of French teenagers. *Why can't talking be as easy as a kiss?* Casey thought, as Madame LeCombe's raspy three-pack-a-day voice crowded into her brain—along with all her uncertainty.

after-school
special

Sophie stretched her legs out on the oversized coffee-colored leather sofa in the oak-paneled St. John family room, absent-mindedly fondling the remote with one hand, a Diet Pepsi sweating in the other. The first day back at school always made her want to veg out on the couch for at least a few hours . . . or days. Anything was better than locking herself in her room to tackle the immense pile of homework she'd lugged home in her Vuitton satchel. She was probably going to develop a hernia before she even lost her virginity . . .

Homework on the first day is so totally passé, Sophie thought, switching over to MTV where Ludacris was jumping around with a bottle of Cristal in one hand, and a girl encased in the typical video-ho gear of tight, faded jeans and ridiculously high stiletto heels in the other. The video slut's outfit was a far cry from the Calvin Klein tank and Juicy shorts Sophie had changed into the minute she arrived home from school. Sophie studied the TV, pensively tilting her head back and downing the last of her Diet Pepsi as her father, Alistair St. John, walked into the room, followed closely by Sophie's mother, Phyllis. Sophie sat up, folding her legs beneath her.

"What are you guys doing home so early?" she wondered aloud as her mother sat down across from her in a leather chair upholstered in varying shades of tan and cognac, and crossed her long, still-shapely legs. Her parents never came home this early. Phyllis St. John—otherwise known as the Upper East Side's own Angelina Jolie—was on the board of directors of UNICEF and the Fresh Air Fund, and when she wasn't busy saving the planet by orchestrating elaborate fund-raisers at the Waldrof-Astoria or the Ritz, she spent most of her nights at the French Culinary Institute, where she'd recently enrolled in a series of gourmet cooking classes. For her mom to even set foot in The Bram before nine P.M. was seriously weird—but not as strange as the fact that her father was currently standing in front of her.

Alistair St. John was a wildly successful real estate mogul whose career was largely built on the fact that his firm had "revitalized" the East Village, clearing out all the starving artists in the early nineties and erecting a series of ubermodern glass-and-steel apartment buildings. Her dad usually spent his days in complicated lunch meetings with Donald Trump, only to come home and immediately begin torturing her mother with just how gorgeous Trump's new wife, Melania, was. But today her father didn't look like he was in any mood for joking as he began pacing the length of the Bokhara rug in cream and beige that dominated the St. John family room, his salon-tanned forehead a mass of wrinkles no amount of Botox could smooth out.

"What's going on?" Sophie asked nervously, noticing the worried look on her mother's face.

"We've got something big to discuss with you, Sophie honey," her mother said, and Sophie noticed that her mother looked almost pale underneath her olive complexion and the deep tan she cultivated year round. *Oh crap*, Sophie thought, exhaling. *They got the last American Express bill.* She didn't mean to go so over the top, really she didn't. Okay, so she did go shopping almost every other day for the past month—but, then again, she couldn't be expected to wear the same four bikinis every week at the rooftop pool at the Soho House, now could she? And that went double for her family's house on Martha's Vineyard, where she'd spent most of June and July mooning over Will, the cute townie who clipped their vast rows of hedges. Having a thing for the gardener was so *Lady Chatterley's Lover*. Sophie had given a report on D. H. Lawrence last year in English class, where she'd argued that in the twenty-first century Lady Chatterley would've been known as a "playa," and that anyone who disliked the book was an anti-feminist who liked to "playa hate." Needless to say, it didn't go over too well with her English teacher, Mrs. Williams, who looked like she could benefit from a lusty romp with the gardener herself . . .

"Sophie," her mother began in the World Peace Now! voice she liked to use when giving elaborate speeches, "you're turning sixteen soon, and there's something rather serious we need to discuss."

At the mention of her impending birthday, Sophie felt herself relax. So *that's* what this was all about—they probably wanted to talk to her about the party. Trouble was, the plans for that party were a done deal: They'd already hired one of the Upper East Side's premiere event planners to take care of every last detail, *and* reserved space at Marquee. So, what else was there to talk about? Phoebe and Madison had already turned sixteen months ago, and Sophie thought she'd die waiting for the chance to upstage them. Ever since her sixth-grade English teacher had discovered Sophie plowing through the complete works of Jane Austen and recommended to her parents that she skip a grade, she'd felt out of step with the rest of her classmates in more ways than one. Watching Phoebe and Mad turn sixteen last year while she had to wait for a whole new school year to arrive had been completely unbearable. If she had known that falling for Mr. Darcy would cause this much trouble, she would've been sure to have kept Jane a secret and made *sure* her teachers saw her reading nothing but Stephen King—that way they might've even left her *back* a year, so she could turn sixteen before everyone else. Sophie wrapped her arms around her torso, hugging herself happily. Maybe they were going to spill the details of her present early! The corners of Sophie's bow-shaped lips turned up in a smile as she pictured a silver Ferrari, a bright pink ribbon wound around its shining metallic hood parked out in front of The Bram—and the look of envy clouding Madison's face as Sophie slid into the driver's seat . . .

". . . that's why we waited to tell you . . . adoption . . . biological mother."

Sophie's head came up like a hunting dog, and she stared at her mother uncomprehendingly. Phyllis smoothed down her Carolina Herrera beige linen pants, the thick gold Chanel cuffs on both wrists sparkling in the late-afternoon sunlight. Sophie noticed that all of a sudden it felt like she was breathing way too fast, and she put one hand on her heart to make sure it was still there, knocking around wildly in her chest.

"Tell me *what*?" Sophie said, feeling the tight muscle of her heart racing beneath her palm. "Adoption? What are you guys *talking* about?"

"Sophie," her father said, his three-button silk suit looking just as crisp as when he'd put it on at five that morning, his dark beard neatly trimmed. "We adopted you when you were just six months old. Your mother and I didn't think . . ." Alistair broke off, looking helplessly at her mother, his mouth opening and closing. Phyllis immediately rushed to fill in the gap, her voice hurried and nervous.

"What your father's trying to say, Sophie, honey, is that we didn't think I could get pregnant again—after Jared we tried and tried and . . . nothing." Her mother looked at the floor, and cleared her throat delicately. "So we adopted you. There was a woman in my acting class—we became friends and then she got pregnant . . ." Her mother's voice trailed off and she stared down at the carpet, a pensive expression darkening her features.

"Since when were you an actress, *Mom*?" Sophie wondered aloud, feeling like her entire world had just messily imploded all over the living room rug.

"It was something I tried out before you were born," her mother said. "I was never very serious—nor very good." Phyllis looked up at Sophie pleadingly, her pain contorting her expression. "But your . . . Melissa—well, she was very good— I think she knew even then that she was going to have a big career."

"So she just . . . gave me to you?" Sophie asked slowly, "like a fucking *sweater*?"

"Watch your language, young lady," her father snapped, crossing his arms over his chest, clearly uncomfortable with the trajectory of the conversation. "Yes," he continued, "she allowed us to adopt you—but there were . . . conditions."

"What conditions?" Sophie demanded. She felt like the whole world had suddenly been tilted on its side, and everything in her once-normal life was now flipped completely upside down. Things were moving way too fast and her stomach turned over like a Russian gymnast on crank. She felt scarily nauseated.

"We promised your birth mother that, when you turned sixteen, we'd tell you that you were adopted—and that we'd allow her to meet you, *if* you wanted to," Phyllis added nervously, twisting the Fred Leighton diamond-and-emerald white-gold eternity ring Sophie's father had surprised her with as a fortieth birthday present last month so relentlessly that her finger would probably come popping off at any minute, blood spurting out all over the carpet, which was worth more than most people's New York apartments. "You certainly don't *have* to meet her," she added, smiling hopefully.

"Why didn't she want to keep in touch with me—or *you*?" Sophie demanded, trying desperately to make sense of the thoughts flooding her brain like a monsoon. Her body felt at once both tingly and numb, and she had that pukey, sweaty feeling—like she'd drank one too many cappuccinos at lunch. She stared uncomprehendingly at the TV as Jay-Z moved around a preening Beyoncé, throwing his hands in the air.

"She got busy with her career," her mother said quietly. "And we all agreed it would be best for you to have a . . . fresh start."

"You agreed," Sophie said woodenly, "without even asking me." It was a statement, not a question, and as she sat there trying desperately to focus on what her parents were telling her, despite her obvious confusion, Sophie was aware of the fact that suddenly, all her past feelings of incompleteness made perfect sense. Her life was exactly like one of those stupid optical illusion paintings they sold in mall in the suburbs—not that Sophie had ever been to the suburbs, much less walked the hideous confines of a mall—where a series of squiggly lines suddenly became a glowing silver dolphin if you looked at it the right way. And once you knew the hidden image was there, it was impossible to view the picture the same way ever again.

Sophie stood up, her body shaking with rage, her fists

clenched at her sides. Her whole life up until now had been nothing more than one enormous *lie*.

With his usual impeccable timing, Jared sauntered into the room bare-chested, shoving the last of her personal stash of chocolate-chocolate chip Häagen-Dazs she'd hidden in the back of the freezer last week into his open mouth.

"What's going on?" Jared scraped the bottom of the carton with a spoon, and flopped down on the couch, grabbing the remote.

"We're talking to Sophie, dear," Phyllis said, standing up and running a hand through her dark, chin-length bob. "And shouldn't you be working on your college applications?"

"Uh, yeah," Jared said, his mouth full. "That's a great idea, Mom. You know—considering I just got kicked out of Exeter and everything. I'm sure Ivy League schools will be lining up to admit me."

"Jared," her father began, his voice like steel, "you have got to get serious. You can't go surfing through life as if there aren't any consequences. When I was your age . . ."

From somewhere far away, Sophie could hear her father droning on about "responsibility" and "choices," as she watched her brother put his dirty feet up on the couch and lean back, scraping the last dregs of chocolate ice cream from the now-empty carton while she just stood there, being totally ignored. Couldn't this moment be about *her* for once? She'd just received the most potentially life-changing information in all of her almost-sixteen years—and now all anyone wanted to talk about was Jared's dumbass college applications, as if any university in its right mind would ever accept him anyway. Sophie tightened her fists, digging her nails into her palms and wondered how long she could stand there, feeling invisible. If she didn't say something soon, smoke would start pouring out of her ears like in the cartoons she still watched on random Saturday mornings.

"How could you *lie* to me?" she screamed at her parents, tears falling from her green eyes and streaming down her face, smearing the Urban Decay bronzer she'd applied that morning into ugly brown streaks.

"Oh, Sophie," her mother said, her face falling. "It's more complicated than that, honey. We just—"

"You just *what*?" Sophie screamed, tears running down her face. "You just decided that it would be more convenient to *lie* to me for my entire life until now? Is that it?" Her parents just stood there silently—even Jared stopped licking the ice-cream carton and just sat there, mouth open. Sophie could feel her nose snotting all over her upper lip, and she wiped it away with the back of her hand, not caring how gross it was as she ran out of the room and down the long hallway, slamming her bedroom door behind her and sinking to her knees on the plush carpet.

Out of the corner of her eye she saw her pink razor lying on the counter of her white-and-turquoise tiled bathroom. She wanted more than anything to pop the blade from the casing and draw it roughly across her skin until she couldn't feel much of anything at all. But she knew that it wouldn't solve any of her problems. She'd feel better for the moment, sure, but tomorrow morning she'd feel just as bad and the cycle would start all over again. And maybe she was looking at this all the wrong way. Okay, so her biological mother may have given her up, and her parents may have lied to her, but now, at least, she knew the truth—and that meant she had options.

Sophie stood up and then sat at her desk in front of her titanium MacBook. She pulled up Google and plugged in her own name, but all she got was a passing mention in an online society rag, and some weird girl's blog talking about how hot Jared was. Gross.

Jared had always teased her about being adopted, but it had never seriously crossed her mind that it really might be true. Sophie sat back in her chair and crossed her bare legs beneath her, Indian style, her eyes drawn to the framed photograph on her desk of her family at Jared's lacrosse game last year, her blond hair shining brightly out of the picture like a beacon—or a signal to pay attention. Why had she never really considered it? And would having a brand-new family be so bad? It's not like she got along so well with her own anyway. And her real mom could be anyone. Hadn't Phyllis said that her mother had been an actress? Maybe her real mom was someone truly fabulous— even though she obviously needed her head examined for giving up a daughter as amazing as Sophie. Whatever the reason, Sophie knew that she wanted to find out. And maybe, just maybe, for the first time ever she just might end up somewhere she really belonged . . .

back
to
basics

Drew sat in his room, staring at the blank white screen
of his laptop and nursing an imported Dutch beer. Why were
girls so weird? He thought that he and Casey were getting
along pretty well before she'd practically attacked him in
French class. By the time lunch had rolled around, he could
barely look at her, and he'd prayed that she'd get the hint and
stay on the other end of the Dining Hall with Mad, Phoebe,
and Sophie—where she belonged. Still, each time he'd looked
up and caught her staring at him with that sad, mournful look,
he'd felt kind of bad. Tomorrow, he was definitely going out
for some Ray's sausage and mushroom pizza—his favorite—
and avoiding all the potential drama.

Drew exhaled heavily and took another swallow of beer. It

kind of sucked—he'd had this whole Woody Allen–type fantasy of showing Casey around the city, maybe taking her at sunset to that spot where Woody and Diane Keaton had their first almost-date, sitting on the bench overlooking the Manhattan Bridge, watching the sunrise. As they'd stood there in the Dining Hall talking so effortlessly, he could almost see her curly hair resting lightly on his shoulder as they looked into the changing sky, the lights coming on across the bridge like a strand of Christmas lights . . .

Too bad it was never going to happen—girls who hung all over him were always a turnoff. No matter how pretty she was, or how into her he might be, when girls started throwing themselves at him it always just seemed kind of desperate. And, to be honest, it made him kind of nervous, too. What was he supposed to do when some girl ran her hand up and down his arm in front of the whole class? Kiss her? Throw her to the floor and rip off her clothes? Actually, that wasn't sounding like such a bad idea all of a sudden . . .

Drew drained the last dregs of beer from the amber bottle and tossed it in the trash as a Gchat message flashed across the blank screen.

socialiez666: What up?

Drew paused before answering, his fingers hovering over the keyboard, a smile creeping across his face. It was so totally predictable—why fight it? He and Madison couldn't seem to stay away from one another, no matter how much they pissed each other off. Come to think of it, they'd never really given things a serious shot—they'd always just hooked up and pretended it didn't really happen the day after. Maybe he should really try and see what happened. The only problem was, when he looked at Mad, as gorgeous as she was, he didn't really get that *feeling*, those crazy butterflies everyone talked about in the movies. Sure, he wanted to tear off her dress and eat it for breakfast, but it wasn't like he spent his nights thinking about holding her hand and watching the sunset. But maybe that was because, except for that disastrous night before he left for Amsterdam, he'd never really *tried*.

dva1990: Not much. Wanna hang tomorrow night?

The Gchat window stayed motionless, the icon blinking for what felt like forever. Drew realized that he was holding his breath waiting for her response. All of a sudden he was completely terrified that she might say no. Madison was as much of a constant in his life as his parents—or that chair in the corner. He couldn't even for a minute imagine his life without her in it. And if that wasn't love, than what was? Probably something best described by Jerry Springer . . .

socialiez666: K ☺ Talk later.

Drew logged off, breathing a sigh of relief and stood up, stretching his long arms above his head and stretching his muscles until he heard his back crack, unlocking the tension in his spine he'd been carrying around all day. Maybe, despite what his dad or anyone else said, it was just easier to continue playing it safe—and for Drew Van Allen, Madison Macallister was about as safe as it got. In a way, it was effortless—Mad was the girl everyone expected him to be with, the most beautiful girl in school from the most notorious family on the entire Upper East Side. But that was exactly the problem—Drew had never been the kind of guy who did what was expected of him—in fact, once he knew that he was supposed to do something—or someone—he usually did the polar opposite, and ran as fast as his feet could carry him in the other direction.

If he was totally honest with himself, Drew knew that he'd never really taken Mad seriously as actual girlfriend material—when they weren't making out frantically, they were more like an old married couple who argued and bickered all the time than anything resembling the kind of great love stories he sometimes caught on late-night TV—if he was Bogie, Madison was definitely not Bacall. The problem was that they were so set in this ridiculous pattern of fighting, then making up—or out—that the whole thing had gotten pretty old. Maybe they needed to bust out of their comfort zone and do something that would take their relationship to a different level—one where they couldn't argue all the time—or tear each other's clothes off either.

Not that total nakedness with Madison was necessarily a bad idea . . .

owner
of a
lonely
heart

☭

Casey sat cross-legged on her bed, surveying the open textbooks that surrounded her like an ocean of slick, glossy paper. She'd never really experienced the pressure of having to exceed academically before. Back in Normal, no one really paid much attention to her test scores or eventual report card except for her mother, who would usually use Casey's grades as an excuse to start waxing ecstatic about the merits of "applying one-self in an academic setting." It was hard not to yawn when Barbara really got going, but Casey had learned to plaster an engaged expression on her face, nodding periodically as though she were actually listening, when in reality she was usu-ally entertaining a series of completely random thoughts—like what the probability would be of getting her hair to grow back in magically straight if she buzzed it all off with a pair of clippers like Britney Spears in the throes of her nineteenth nervous breakdown . . .

It's not that she didn't care about doing well—it's just that, before now, she'd never had to particularly *try* very hard. No offense to her former Illinois classmates, but the kids back home were more interested in planning the next kegger and cruising Main Street on Saturday nights than they were in studying for the dreaded SATs. Class was for passing notes and daydreaming—not for raising your hand or, God forbid, actually paying *attention*. But at Meadowlark, she had to fight just to get a word in during class discussions, which could only be described as *intense*. To add a little more pressure, keeping her grades up was one of the conditions of her continued enrollment. If she wanted to stay at Meadowlark, good grades weren't a choice—they were a necessity. The thing that unnerved her the most about her new school was the feeling that she wasn't allowed to screw up, even if she wanted to. As she sat in class after class, listening to her fellow students give intricate, detailed explanations of the Crimean war and global warming, Casey started to wonder if too much perfection was really a good thing. It wasn't the pressure to excel that was really bothering her—it was the fact that being a Meadowlark student meant that she flat-out wasn't *allowed* to make mistakes. And that made her nervous indeed.

After a full day of French, Trigonometry, History, and Sociology, Casey's brain hurt, her eyes glazing over as she mindlessly flipped through her French workbook. *I probably have drain bramage from reading too much*, she thought, closing her sore eyes and rubbing her temples with her index fingers. Not that she could study even if she wanted to—not after the way Drew acted after she'd practically attacked him. Casey flipped open her battered Sprint phone and checked for missed calls . . . again. Predictably, there weren't any. She snapped the phone shut and threw it to the end of the bed, where it landed with a thump, and picked up her violin from the floor, running her hands over the taut strings. Sometimes just holding the rich, reddish-brown-hued wood seemed reassuring—and right now she needed all the reassurance she could get.

She couldn't stop thinking about the look on Drew's face when she ran her hand up his arm—and the look that must've been all over her own when he had pulled away. And later that afternoon as he passed by her in the hallway, he just smiled, waved . . . and kept walking. She thought he would at least stop, say hi, and maybe ask how her day was going—but the way he waved so nonchalantly, his smile so tight, made it clear that stopping to talk, or calling her later was the last thing on his mind. Was she not aggressive *enough*? Casey couldn't help but entertain the sneaking suspicion that maybe she'd be better off simply ignoring Madison's dating advice. Why did making friends have to be so hard here? Back home in Normal, hanging out with her friends had been effortless, but since she'd arrived at The Bram, Casey couldn't help but have the feeling that no matter how hard she tried to get along with Mad, no matter what she said or did, it wouldn't make any difference. Why couldn't they all just be friends without guys getting in the way?

Umm, maybe because you're in lust with her ex-boyfriend, her inner pragmatist answered back matter-of-factly . . .

Casey sighed, placing her violin gently back on the floor and lying back on the blue quilt. The fabric emitted a noxious combination of mothballs and the Chanel N° 5 Nanna had obviously sprayed all over it in an attempt to mask the hideous, medicinal scent. It was probably too much to hope for that the most gorgeous guy she'd ever seen would pick her over someone like Madison Macallister. Why couldn't things be like they were in the movies, where the least popular girl always got the hottest guy in school? Casey sat up and opened her new laptop, popping her *Pretty in Pink* DVD into the side slot. There was no mistaking it—Drew was Andrew McCarthy to her (she hoped) slightly better-dressed Molly Ringwald, the girl from the wrong side of the tracks. Or maybe just the wrong floor. All she wanted was to cut to the final scene where they overcame their class differences and made out in the school parking lot after the prom . . .

Wait, Meadowlark didn't even *have* a parking lot. Or a prom. A prom was a little passé when you've been spending most of your weekends since you were thirteen shuttling between Marquee and some exclusive party at the Met. Casey pulled her hair into a curly mop on top of her head, securing it with a rubber band. Okay, then, in her fantasy Drew would grab her in the Dining Hall, pressing his body to hers in front of the salad bar, the steel tongs glinting in the light, his lips lightly brushing her own, the mouthwatering scent of organic bacon cheeseburgers in the air . . .

A sharp rap on the bedroom door snapped Casey out of her decidedly PG-rated thoughts, and she hit the spacebar to pause the movie. "Can I come in?" Nanna called as she pushed the door open and walked in before Casey could answer. Nanna was dressed for what she called "a night on the town," in a silvery-gray cocktail dress that looked like it'd been buried in a time capsule in 1965 and dug up that morning. The triple-strand of creamy pearls she always wore on special occasions hung around her neck, and pearl-gray leather pumps encased her feet. Her legs shone with the gleam of sheer silk stockings, and her face was bare but for a dusting of light face powder and a slash of petal-pink lipstick Casey knew was called Antique Rose, because it was the only shade Nanna ever wore.

"I hope you're not wearing that getup for me," Casey said, smiling as her grandmother pirouetted once, showing off her outfit from all angles. "Because I have to hit the books tonight if I'm going to have a shot in hell at keeping up at this fancy-pants school."

"Not unless your name happens to be Arthur—and you're a retired captain in the Air Force!" Nanna cackled, her eyes glittering, and Casey wondered for the millionth time how somebody so old could possibly have so much energy. Nanna stepped in front of the mirror hanging over the bed and smoothed down her silvery bob. Genetics weren't fair. How was it that Nanna was blessed with stick-straight hair while everyone else in the McCloy family had to contend with locks that looked more like a tangled mass of spaghetti than anything remotely resembling the hair of an actual human being?

"So, how was the first day?" Nanna asked, sitting down on the edge of the bed, arranging the silky fabric of her skirt with one hand so she wouldn't wrinkle. "Brutal, I take it?"

"That would be one way of describing it." Casey pulled her hair down and scratched her head with both hands, her brain pounding in her skull. Not only was her hair a nightmare to deal with on a daily basis, every time she put it up the sheer mass of it gave her an instant migraine.

"You want to talk about brutal?" Nanna pointed at the slim Cartier watch on her wrist, tapping the worn mother-of-pearl face with one antique, rose-polished fingernail. "In exactly forty minutes, I'll be sitting at Tavern on the Green, trying to look interested as Arthur drones on about planes and flight specifications while fussy waiters call me ma'am and try to run away with my plate before I've finished eating."

"Yeah, that sounds just awful." Casey smiled. "Being forced to eat an expensive three-course meal in a gorgeous restaurant in the middle of Central Park." Casey rolled her gray eyes and smiled. "Arthur is your date, I take it? And a pilot, too? Wow, Nanna," Casey lay back on the bed, her arms under her head, "my heart really bleeds for you."

"*Was* a pilot, Miss Smarty-Pants," Nanna said, standing up and smacking Casey on the hip with the palm of one hand. "He's retired—or haven't you been paying attention?"

Ow. Nanna's skeleton hands hurt when she got feisty. Casey rolled her eyes, rubbed her hip, and glared at the ceiling. It was so depressing. Here she was sitting home by herself feeling like the biggest loser on the planet, and even her *grandmother* had a hot date. Okay, well maybe not exactly *hot*, but at least it was an actual *date*.

"Well, have fun," Casey said with a sigh. "Don't stay out too late."

"No need to worry about *that*," Nanna scoffed. "These old guys are used to falling asleep in their chairs in front of the TV by ten o'clock—I'll be lucky if he makes it past the appetizers!" Nanna cackled again, cracking herself up, then placing her hands on her hips, she peered at Casey as though at any minute she might turn into a bug straight out of a Kafka story. "Casey Anne McCloy, are you just going to mope around here all night long?"

"Probably," Casey moaned. "My life is a disaster. And don't call me Casey Anne—it makes me sound like one of the fringe characters in *Deliverance*."

"How can your life be a disaster?" Nanna demanded while walking to the door and placing one hand on the knob. "You just *got* here!"

"Exactly," Casey said, sitting back up and closing her laptop. "It's a *talent* I have—making a mess out of my life in forty-eight short hours . . ."

"You kids these days are so *dramatic*." Nanna rolled her eyes and glanced quickly at her watch. "Why don't you open that thing up"—Nanna pointed to Casey's closed laptop—"and kill a few hours on YouSpace or MyTube?"

Casey burst out laughing, drawing her knees up and hugging them to her chest. "Nanna, its *My*Space and You*Tube*."

Casey stopped laughing and looked at Nanna incredulously. "And how do you know about stuff like that anyway?"

"Casey, honey," Nanna said, a mischievous look in her blue eyes, "I'm old—I'm not dead." Nanna pulled the door open and waved over her shoulder, a powdery, scented cloud of Chanel N° 5 trailing behind her. "Don't wait up!" she called out before shutting the door firmly. The metal clicking of the locks turning sounded like a cell door closing—and from the sorry state of Casey's New York love life, she was clearly being sentenced to a lifetime in unpopular, dateless Loserville.

Casey opened her laptop and logged onto MySpace, plugging Drew's name into the Search feature. When his page came up, featuring a picture of Drew, sunburned and screamingly cute, sitting on some very Euro-looking bridge with a cluster of boats and barges in the background, she felt more depressed than ever. Especially when she noticed that Drew had more than one thousand friends, while Casey's page, embarrassing as it was to admit, only had a hundred—tops. It was official: She was clearly a friendless loser. Even Nanna was out getting wined and dined, and here she was sitting in her room, mooning over some guy's MySpace page.

Ugh, Casey thought, tracing the contours of Drew's face with the pad of her index finger, *it's a pretty sad state of affairs when your grandmother's love life is hotter than your own . . .*

date night

✦

Madison held tightly onto Drew's hand as he helped her out of a cab on the Lower East Side. She couldn't believe she'd actually agreed to this—coming all the way downtown just to eat Mexican food at some ridiculous restaurant at the bottom of a fucking *vault*—but here she was, stepping out of a cab, her new black patent leather Manolos landing squarely in a puddle as a late summer shower rained down on their heads.

Drew had wisely waited to inform her that they were heading downtown until *after* she'd stepped into the cab and he'd presented her with a single gorgeous white lily, his dimple wrinkling adorably. It wasn't like Madison had anything *against* downtown, really, but she had nothing *for* it either.

Besides, it wasn't like the Upper East Side was exactly suffering from a lack of great restaurants—there was really no reason to ever come down to this haven for hipsters, poseurs, and trust-fund junkies. *Ever*.

"Come on!" Drew shouted over the downpour, his fingers closing tightly around her own as he pulled her across the street toward the restored steel dining car on the corner, the thunder cracking loudly above their heads. *Fucking great*, Madison thought, reaching up and patting her hair with her free hand. She'd spent two hours putting it up, securing every last wayward, blond strand, and now it was completely soaked through—along with her black silk Diane von Furstenberg wrap dress. As they stood under the huge red neon sign that proclaimed La Esquina, catching their breath, Madison couldn't help but feel a little pissed off as she surveyed the wreckage of her outfit—a look that took her hours to put together. This was supposed to be their makeup date, and she looked like a drowned rat. *Attractive*, Madison muttered under her breath, reaching up and pulling the pins from her hair, shaking it around her shoulders in a rain-soaked frizzy mess.

Madison peered inside the plate-glass windows of the dining car in disbelief, taking in the fast-food counter, the fluorescent lighting, and the hungry crowds munching away on beef tacos. Where was the candlelight, the chilled white wine, the white linen tablecloths and soft music? Who did he think she was anyway—Casey?

"You've got to be kidding me, Drew!" Madison erupted

angrily. "You dragged me all the way downtown in the pour-ing rain to eat at a *taco joint*? My dress is ruined!"

"It's just a little rain, Mad. It's not going to kill you." An annoyed expression crossed Drew's face and he brushed his wet hands off on his Seven jeans, and straightened his black Paul Smith blazer.

No, Madison thought, silently thanking God that she was wearing waterproof mascara, *but I just might . . .*

"And I told you—it's not *just* a taco joint. Come *on*." Drew grabbed her hand again, and against her better judgment she allowed him to lead her around the side of the building, the rain pelting her in the face to a battered gray door marked EMPLOYEES ONLY.

"What are you *doing*? We can't go in there!" Madison grabbed his wrist as he pulled the door open. Had he suddenly lost his mind? Or maybe all of his IQ points had just been washed away in the torrential rain flooding the streets.

"It's cool," Drew tossed nonchalantly over his shoulder, "I promise." Madison sighed and followed Drew into the building, and down a dark set of sinister-looking stairs that were a serious fucking challenge if you were lucky enough to be wearing flip-flops—much less Manolos. When they came out into the light, Madison blinked her eyes at the sudden shock of overhead lighting illuminating what could only be the restaurant's kitchen. Mexican cooks wearing chef jackets paid them absolutely no attention as they busily worked the grill, the smell of onions and chilies perfuming the air.

"This way," Drew said authoritatively, leading her through

a maze of hallways that ended abruptly with at a thick steel door fronted by a sleek black podium, a small pin light attached to the top. The podium looked completely out of place, considering the exceedingly sewerlike surroundings. Behind it stood a rail-thin bouncer, tightly gripping the black square of a clipboard, the white of his hands and face standing out in stark contrast to the darkness of the hall. Drew walked up to the podium, lightly clearing his throat, but the bouncer didn't budge, and continued to stare at the clipboard like it was the most fascinating thing he'd ever seen. Drew cleared his throat again, this time loud enough for the sound to echo off the dank walls.

"What is this, fucking Madame Tussauds?" Madison whispered. The bouncer let out a small chuckle.

"If this is a wax museum, then you two must be some bridge-and-tunnel types, looking for a big, bad night on the town." He still hadn't raised his eyes from the clipboard.

"Don't mind her," Drew said, leaning forward onto the podium, "we're here for the menudo. I hear it's tremendous." Madison's exquisitely manicured fingernail dug into his shoulder as she squeezed out her anger.

"Menudo? I thought this was a restaurant, not a concert venue for some tired Latin pop group."

"Mad, please . . ."

"Menudo on Sundays only. You'll have to come back."

"Just give us a table," Drew said, "we'll drink until midnight. And I know you guys start stewing that tripe on Friday." A look of surprise briefly crossed the bouncer's face.

Madison smirked with satisfaction. Dating a guy whose father was in the restaurant business often came in handy at places like this.

"I see—so you're a bridge-and-tunneler who trolls eGullet for lack of anything better to do," the bouncer said dryly, his eyes drifting back to the clipboard, shoulders relaxing, shutting off all body signals for future communication.

"Are you really going to make me recite all twenty-six ingredients in the shrimp ceviche?" Drew said with an eyebrow raised. "Or can we just cut to the part where you show us to our table before I have to get my father on the phone. His name's Robert Van Allen. Maybe you've heard of him?"

The bouncer snapped to attention, the light glinting off the lenses of his glasses, obscuring his expression.

"Wait—you're a Van Allen? Um, Okay. Let me see." The bouncer looked down at his clipboard and crossed through a name with his red pen just as another couple stepped into the dark of the hallway and out of the bright lights of the kitchen.

"Excuse me, we have a reservation," the man said timidly, adjusting his gold, wire-rimmed round glasses with one plump, pink hand.

"Good for you—tell the whole world," the bouncer said over his shoulder, giving their Birkenstocks and tie-dyed T-shirts a disdainful look, "but you're not eating dinner here tonight." The couple stood there for a moment in shock, mouths open, before turning around and walking back toward the steel door.

"Okay, Van Allen," the bouncer said, giving Madison's legs

the once-over, "follow me." Madison trailed behind Drew as they meandered through the narrow hallway, ending up in a large, cavernous room decorated with dripping wrought-iron candelabras, imposing-looking metal gates adorning the walls.

"Wow," Madison whispered, taking in the couples draped in Prada and Fendi seated at small tables scattered throughout the room, coolly watching over their large white menus as Madison and Drew were led to a table in the back. "I thought you were *kidding* when you said it was a vault."

"What exactly were you expecting?" the bouncer snorted, pulling out Madison's chair, "a décor reminiscent of your local suburban Taco Bell?" Madison rolled her eyes and picked up her menu as the bouncer slunk away—presumably to torture more patrons.

"So," she said, smiling over the top of the menu and trying to be a good sport even though she felt about as sexy as a wet cat. Whatever—the wet look was totally back in . . . as of now. Madison swept her sopping hair off her shoulders and surveyed the dungeonesque interior. Her soggy dress notwithstanding, she couldn't be *too* mad about the situation. Drew had definitely gone to a lot of trouble to get them in . . . even if the restaurant was practically around the corner from the ninth circle of hell— otherwise known as the LES—and had a stricter door policy than Bungalow. "What's good here?"

"My dad says the ceviche is really good." Drew perused the menu thoughtfully. "Also, the red snapper and the cilantro- lime sorbet."

Twenty minutes later, after a black leather–clad waitress

scribbled down their order in a way that personified bitchy, Madison was on her second margarita and was feeling no pain as she sipped at the salty, tequila-laced concoction. She loved margaritas—it was like drinking almost frozen, slightly salty lemonade, only better. As she stared at Drew's tanned face in the candlelight, she wondered if she was being too petty about everything. Okay, so he hadn't called her this summer—or written. And maybe their first time *was* a complete disaster, but when he smiled at her across the table, reaching out to clasp her hand in his and tickling her palm with slow, catlike strokes that made her want to curl up in the sun, purring like a kitty—all of a sudden the past just didn't seem to matter anymore. *Yeah, right,* her inner bitch snapped, *that's definitely the tequila talking . . .*

"So, what are you doing this weekend?" Drew asked as their appetizer of foie gras tacos arrived. "I thought I might go see the new Aldomóvar flick—if you want to come."

Madison's fork hovered in the air, and she shot Drew a look like he was seriously disturbed, her green eyes narrowing.

"Subtitles?" she moaned. "Aldomóvar? You must be kidding." Madison put her fork down at the side of her plate decisively. "Haven't we already had this conversation?"

"Yeah, but . . ." Drew protested before she held up a hand in front of his face, palm out, cutting him off.

"I know these pretentious art films are like your only reason for *living* and everything." Madison picked up the fork again, this time plunging it into the mound of refried beans falling out of the taco. "But we do enough reading at *school*, Drewster. And there's no way I'm sitting in the dark for two hours in some stinky arthouse theater. Movies are supposed to be watched anyway—not read!"

"*Some* movies," Drew muttered, taking a large bite of taco and chewing loudly, a decidedly sullen expression replacing the happy grin he'd worn only moments before. Well, tough titty. She'd put up with a lot from Drew, but she really had to draw the line at foreign films . . .

"Or there's this show at the Guggenheim that my mom told me about," Drew said spearing a piece of charred onion and popping it into his mouth.

An art show? Madison raised one eyebrow—all those hours practicing in front of the mirror were definitely worth it—and swallowed a mouthful of ground pork. Madison knew how the day would turn out. Drew would drag her around some over air-conditioned, dusty museum, pointing out the great masterworks of avant-garde art and explaining the surrealist movement or some other dumb bullshit, when she could be out shopping the annual Jimmy Choo sale like a normal person. No, thank you.

"Well, it was just an idea," Drew muttered, tilting his bottle of Sol back and swallowing rapidly. Madison smiled, looking down at the now-empty plate. The power of the raised eyebrow was that you could totally negate an idea without ever having to say a word: It was complete genius.

During the main course of herb-stuffed sea bass, Drew looked up from his plate, his eyes serious. "I kind of wanted to talk to you about something," Drew said, taking a deep breath and then coughing loudly, clearing his throat. Drew always got so serious when he tried to get . . . serious—it was one of the things Madison liked best about him. "Before I left . . ." Drew stared down at the table, running one finger along the tight weave of the tablecloth. "I didn't handle things very well . . . with us."

"That's putting it mildly," Madison snapped before she could stop herself. God, why was she such a raging bitch all the time? It was amazing—when Drew was around she always managed to blurt out the worst thing possible. "I'm sorry." Madison exhaled loudly. "I've just been a little . . . confused— all this time." Once the words left her lips, she knew they were true, and before she could stop them by thinking of something sarcastic to say, her eyes welled up with tears. She really hated having emotions in public—it made her feel all exposed and oogey—as if she was sitting in front of the whole room in nothing but her pink satin Victoria's Secret thong. Maybe if she kept talking she'd feel better—anything to stop the tears that were threatening to leak out of her eyes at any moment.

"I mean, you didn't even e-mail me. For the whole summer it was like . . . nothing. I almost started feeling like it didn't even happen." She took a deep breath, then looked down at the table, wishing she could just be magically teleported out of her chair and back into her bedroom where she didn't have to suffer this kind of humiliation. *That's right—home's a whole other kind of humiliation* . . .

After Madison had counted the tines on her salad fork at least a hundred times, she finally looked up. Drew was staring back at her, his own eyes shining wetly in the dim light.

"I know, Mad," he said quietly, "and I'm really, really sorry."

As much as she didn't want to, as much as she had trained herself to never allow anyone off the hook with something as easy and simple as an honest, heartfelt apology, she knew that Drew meant it. He was sorry. And even more shocking, she could feel in the pit of her stomach that she was forgiving him—and that *wasn't* the tequila talking.

"Sorry, sorry, sorry. Blah, blah, blah." Madison smiled, taking a gulp of her margarita, trying to brush off the apology with her usual sarcastic banter and the much-needed sting of alcohol. When things got too heavy, she started feeling like there was a scarf wrapped around her neck, pulling tighter and tighter until she couldn't breathe. She hated it—even if the scarf was probably from Hermès . . .

"No, really," Drew said earnestly, leaning forward and resting his elbows on the table. "I was wrong—and I want to make it up to you."

Madison felt herself softening like the cilantro-lime sorbet Drew's dad had recommended. What was he doing to her? Now that he'd apologized, and, better yet, admitted that he was wrong, where could they really go from here? Madison wrinkled her brow, pushing her mostly uneaten fish around on her plate. Even if she did forgive him, was it enough? Her first time was supposed to be something she'd always remember, and there were no do-overs in virginity. She'd never be able to go back in time and fix it. Never.

Madison watched as Drew slid his credit card on top of the check and smiled at her across the table, the dimple in his chin crinkling. When they first started dating, she loved poking that dumb dimple with her finger, tickling him mercilessly so that he'd smile and that small indentation of flesh would appear. Madison played with an almost-dry strand of her hair, curling it around her index finger. She already knew that she wanted him back—and the apology was just icing on the cake. Why was she fighting it?

"You want to make it up to me?" she purred.

"Totally," Drew said as the waitress swooped by like a black leather–clad bird of prey, snatching up the check with her long, black-varnished nails.

"Hmmm." She sighed, her eyes wandering around the room, playing her well-rehearsed "I don't give a fuck" act. Sometimes she wondered when exactly she was going to stop rehearsing all the time, and just be *herself*—whoever that was. "I'll have to think about it, *Andrew,*" she said with a smile and a wink. She might have forgiven him, but that certainly didn't mean that she couldn't continue to torture him. Actually, it seemed all the more appropriate now.

The waitress was back with the check and Drew reached forward to sign it, but Madison was already up, bag in hand and turning toward the door. "But for starters, let's get some Pinkberry . . . I'm *starving.*"

skipping dessert

⊕

Drew wrapped one arm around Madison's nonexistent waist as they walked down Ninety-fourth Street toward the hulking outline of The Bram. He had wanted so much to impress her with La Esquina—and the food *was* really good—but she'd hardly touched her plate. Whatever—he'd seen this routine before more times than he could count. Madison's idea of eating was cutting her food up into tiny, bite-sized pieces and pushing them around on her plate until the whole mess looked more like abstract art than a tasty meal. It was kind of ridiculous: He was the son of one of New York's most well-known chefs, and he was dating a girl who didn't eat. Adding insult to injury was the fact that Madison thought Pinkberry frozen yogurt and vanilla lattes were basically two of the four food groups.

"Did I tell you what happened between Phoebe and that boy she met this summer out in the Hamptons?" Madison asked, taking a bite of the so-called frozen yogurt, which they had waited on line two hours for. Pinkberry was almost harder to get a taste of than the tacos at La Esquina. "Well, there was this guy she met at the beach and he was, like, totally into Phoebe, and . . ."

Drew nodded along, half pretending to listen and half actually trying to follow along with Madison's story. While her particular brand of cattiness was de rigueur for Madison, Drew was more than familiar with these occasional bouts of girl talk, during which Mad gave a play-by-play reenactment of events occurring at some party or club or beach house or equally fabulous and exclusive place. When he was younger, Drew had always considered being exposed to this kind of blabber a sort of occupational hazard of knowing and dating girls. But as he walked up the street with Madison that night, he found himself wondering if that was the case. There was no doubt in his mind or, um, pants that he was completely, totally, stupidly attracted to Madison and while he had more than a bit to make up for in the in-the-pants department— considering what happened the last time they tried to bump and it got ugly—he was quite certain that the bedroom end of things would improve quickly if they tried again. But this *SophietalkedtoRyanwhotalkedtoJessicawhotalkedtoJohnwhowenttosee Beth* . . . bullshit made him wonder if the epic party in his pants that a mere glimpse of Madison incited was actually worth his while. And she wouldn't watch Almodóvar! If the

line had to be drawn somewhere—and it most certainly did—
wasn't that where to draw it?

Madison stopped talking as she paused on a corner to fix
the strap on her shoe, her slender back arching as she reached
down for the small silver buckle, a streetlight a block behind
throwing her ass and the dipping curve of her hips into silhou-
ette. Drew stopped thinking for a moment . . . and then a few
moments more. The tiniest bit of drool rolled out of the corner of his mouth, as his feet shifted uncomfortably.

"So anyways," Madison went on, "it was this totally crazy
thing because . . ."

Drew was back in the land of the living. Or maybe the land
of the blind or impotent. He wasn't quite sure. *But what's a life
without Woody Allen!* his head screamed. Madison positively
hated Woody Allen. How could he seriously date a girl who
hated practically everything he loved? His pants just shrugged
in reply. They could deal.

Drew, on the other hand, finally decided that he could not.

"Listen, Mad," Drew said, his first words spoken in nearly
five blocks, "I think I'm going to have to call it a night." They
were standing on the sidewalk in front of The Bram, and
Madison had begun to tug expectantly at his hands.

"Nonsense," Madison purred, instantly slipping back into
sex kitten role and pulling Drew in for a kiss. "You just *got*
here." Drew tried to move away, but her arms snaked around
his neck and held on tight. She was smiling and she was gorgeous, her tanned skin glowing in the moonlight, but for the
first time he knew that it wasn't really enough. It was as

picture-perfect a movie moment as he could've hoped for, but Drew couldn't deny the fact that it just didn't feel right. *What are you doing?* the sex-crazed voice inside him called out. *She's the hottest girl on the Upper East Side — maybe all of Manhattan — and you're leaving her out here on the* sidewalk?

Guess so, Drew thought, shifting his weight uneasily, and trying to avoid her green-eyed gaze. *Maybe I'm an idiot,* he thought, looking down at her long, tanned legs and perfect, light pink pedicure. *Okay, I'm* definitely *an idiot, but idiot or not, I don't think I can do this anymore.*

"Really, Mad, I've got to go." Drew said as he pried her arms from his neck and broke away. Without another word, he turned and began to walk very briskly toward home. He didn't dare turn back.

mani, pedi, meltdown

⊜

Sophie leaned back on a pile of burgundy and gold silk pillows at the Jin Soon spa, and sighed luxuriously as a tiny Asian woman with chopsticks protruding from her sleek, dark hair placed Sophie's feet into a basin of warm milk, the scent of raw organic honey drifting across the room. Sophie always felt so relaxed the moment she walked in the door of the tiny salon with its walnut woodwork and gleaming silk, earth-toned pillows and fabrics. The salon was so soothing that she'd probably still come even if the experience was less than amazing—luckily for her, the pedicures were to die for. Besides, Sophie always did some of her best thinking during her weekly mani/pedi while her hands and feet were being massaged with honey and essential oils—and this Saturday was no exception.

Sophie flexed her toes in the hot, fragrant milk and perused the selection of polishes, her hand hovering over OPI's Her Royal Shyness, a light, iridescent pink that looked completely fabulous with a tan and strappy sandals. The weirdest thing about being adopted was how *not* weird it was. Even though the news had been hard to take at first (Okay, that was an understatement), when the word *adopted* fell from her mother's lips, all the disconnected puzzle pieces of her life suddenly fell into place. In a way it was strangely liberating: She didn't have to worry about fitting into her crazy family anymore because they weren't actually her family at all, not biologically. Not that she was speaking to any of them at this moment anyway . . .

The bell on the front door tinkled softly, and Sophie looked up to see Phoebe standing in the doorway wearing a Miss Sixty jean skirt with a Free People orange tank shot through with gold thread, a stack of gold bangle bracelets climbing halfway up her bronzed arm. Phoebe's face lit up when she spied Sophie lounging against the cushions in the back of the room, and she raised her hand, waving happily, her brown eyes shining.

Come over, Sophie mouthed, waving back.

'Kay, Phoebe mouthed back, holding up one index finger in the air while conversing briefly with the receptionist, a thin Asian woman dressed head-to-toe in black linen.

As Phoebe crossed the room, Sophie wondered if she should tell her about being adopted. So far she hadn't told anyone—until today, she really didn't know how she felt about it herself.

Her feelings seemed to change every five minutes, and whenever she thought about meeting her biological mom, her thoughts raced like a socialite in the depths of a cocaine binge. Besides, she wasn't sure that she wanted Madison to find out yet. And Phoebe's only real fault was that she couldn't keep a secret to save her life—either she came right out and told Madison everything, or she was such a bad liar that Madison figured it out, wheedling and whining it out of her in a matter of minutes.

"Hey!" Phoebe said brightly, leaning over to air-kiss Sophie on both cheeks. When she leaned in, Phoebe's shiny, dark hair fell across Sophie's face, and Sophie could smell the familiar scent of Dolce & Gabbana's Light Blue—Phoebe's signature perfume. "I *thought* I might run into you here."

"Well, duh!" Sophie laughed as Phoebe plopped down beside her, pulling off her tangerine Kate Spade ballet flats as Sophie pushed her bangs out of her eyes. "I only come here every Saturday!"

"True dat," Phoebe muttered while choosing her polish, finally settling on The Thrill of Brazil—a hibiscus red that brought out the caramel tones in her tanned skin. "Which pedi should I get?"

"I'm having the milk and honey." Sophie sighed, closing her eyes as her feet were patted dry with a soft terry towel.

'I always get that one," Phoebe said, shaking the bottle of polish vigorously and holding it up to the light.

"That's because it's the best," Sophie said smugly as lavender and vanilla essential oils were massaged onto the soles of her still slightly damp feet.

"Maybe I'll get the Summer Oasis," Phoebe mused as she looked at the list of services on a white, laminated card near the pedicure station. Another tiny Asian woman came out from the back, sitting down at Phoebe's feet and smiling. Sophie wondered if they somehow manufactured them in a storage room or something. They reminded her of the set of Russian dolls her father had brought home for her on his last business trip to St. Petersburg, one fitting snugly inside the next.

"So what are you doing here?" Sophie wondered aloud. "Didn't you just get a pedi on Tuesday?" The bracing scent of mint and cucumber wafted over as Phoebe immersed her feet in a basin of spring water and fresh cucumber slices and mint leaves.

"Yeah," Phoebe said, leaning back on the burgundy cushions, "but I really wanted to get out of the house." Phoebe frowned, bringing her hands up to her temples, massaging her head with her index fingers and closing her eyes.

"Why—what's going on?" Sophie asked, turning her body to face Phoebe. Well, as much as she could with her feet in someone else's hands.

"Nothing," Phoebe muttered. "You know—the usual."

"Are they fighting again?" Sophie asked tentatively as the first sweeping strokes of polish were applied to her toenails. She knew that Phoebe's parents weren't exactly enjoying a second honeymoon recently. The last time she'd hung out at Phoebe's place she could hear the Reynauds arguing halfway down the hallway before she even rang the doorbell. Not that she could understand what they were saying anyway, as they fought both lightning fast and in French. When she'd asked Phoebe about it, Pheebs brushed the whole thing off with a curt, "Don't worry about it," and turned the music up in her bedroom to deafening levels, drowning out the sound of shouting.

"When are they not?" Phoebe said with a sigh. "Don't say anything to Mad, but it's getting really bad lately."

"I won't say anything," Sophie promised, trying her best to look sincere. Although she felt bad for Pheebs, she knew that if Madison asked her point-blank about the Reynauds, Sophie would probably crumble under her unrelenting stare. And, besides, what fun was it hearing other people's darkest secrets if you couldn't ever repeat them? Which was exactly why she wasn't going to tell Phoebe anything about her own completely screwed-up family . . . not yet, anyway.

"So what's going on with them?" Sophie asked as a shiny topcoat was brushed onto her now pearly-pink toenails.

"They just fight all the time—and I really hate that Bijoux has to hear it."

Sophie smiled, picturing Bijoux's round face covered by tiny Versace aviators. "Your sister is *such* a brat."

"Oh, please—it's not like your brother would win any prizes for Sibling of the Year either." Phoebe threw Sophie a look that matched the skepticism in her voice, arching one dark brow as they broke into a mass of giggles.

Sophie rolled her eyes in agreement. "I know—having him home again is a total nightmare."

"Why did he get kicked out of Exeter anyway?"

"Knowing Jared, he probably got the headmaster's wife pregnant or something," Sophie snorted, holding her feet up in front of a tiny, whirring fan. "Or failed Algebra."

"It's so weird," Phoebe mused, "I haven't seen him in, like, two years."

"Lucky for you. I have to see his dumb ass every day—and it killing me. How does everyone expect me to adjust?" Sophie whined, crossing her arms over her chest. "I mean, he's been gone forever, and I've had the place practically to myself. Now he's back, throwing his stinky kicks everywhere, calling me 'bra,' eating all my food, and, worst of all, cluttering up the apartment with his stupid surfing magazines. I didn't even know he could *read*."

"Ugh," Phoebe moaned as her feet were enveloped in a soft towel and rubbed dry. "You're right—it sounds like a nightmare. I officially have no right to be complaining about *anything*. I'm sorry to break it to you, babe," Phoebe said archly, "but your life is a total disaster."

"I know it," Sophie mumbled, slipping her feet into those delicate paper sandals that were the telltale sign of a girl post-pedicure. She knew that Pheebs had been joking, but she found herself wondering if her life really *was* a disaster right now . . . and if it might just be getting worse. The fact that she was adopted certainly answered a lot of questions on her current home front—but what about that other home she had somewhere, the home of her biological mother? With the way things were going lately, why would meeting her bio-mom actually change anything? And what if things just got even *worse*? Even if she met her real mom, that didn't mean they were guaranteed to get along just because they happened to dip into the same gene pool. Plus, she'd be the weird girl with two moms now. Instead of the boring, totally normal family life she'd always thought she had, she'd have this bizarre, fractured family. If she met her bio-mom and they did get along, her life was bound to turn into a made-for-TV movie, where she'd see her real mother once a month on Saturdays or something. And what if her real mother wasn't even single? Then she'd not only have a new mom, but a new stepdad, too . . . Sophie sighed, looking down at her gleaming toes. She could barely handle the family she had—what made her think she'd do any better with a new one?

As Sophie sat there waiting for her toes to dry, a weird prickly sensation came over her, and goosebumps sprung up on her bare arms and legs. As much as she wanted and needed to think positively about the whole situation, and as much as she hoped that her real family would make her feel like she finally fit in, Sophie couldn't help wondering if finally belonging somewhere might just make her feel more like an outsider than ever . . .

love . . .
and
other
bodily fluids

Casey stepped through the revolving doors of the Guggenheim Museum, rolling around twice before finally stumbling out into the frigid air of the lobby. She hated revolving doors with a passion. The only purpose they served, as far as she could tell, was to make her feel even more gawky and uncoordinated than usual. Casey looked up, taking in the gently sloping floor and multilevel, all-white interior, which spiraled up like some sort of bizarre wedding cake. The museum was so cold, clean, and modern that Casey felt like she was encased in ice as she walked to the ticket counter, pulled out a twenty-dollar bill Nanna had slipped her from the back pocket of her much maligned, pink Abercrombie skirt, and handed it to the cashier.

The Guggenheim had one of the largest collections of modern art in the world, and, amazing as the permanent collection was, Casey wasn't exactly kung-fu fighting with the revolving doors on that particular Saturday afternoon due to her undying love for all things artistic. She was there for two reasons. The first reason had to do with her mother calling her last night, specifically to inform Casey of the Kiki Smith retrospective opening today. When Casey had seemed less than enthused, the conversation had degenerated into Barbara screaming that it was her feminist duty to go and get some culture instead of hanging out with a bunch of brainless, bobblehead dolls, wasting her time on manicures, pedicures, or holistic, new-age enema cures. Casey didn't know what was worse—the echo on the transatlantic line, the weirdly Madonnaesque British accent her mother seemed to be developing, or the headache Barbara's diatribe instantly produced in her skull.

"You're less than ten blocks from the greatest modern art museum in the world!" Barbara had shrieked as Casey held her phone away from her ear so that she wouldn't go spontaneously deaf. "Take advantage of it!" And after a glamorous morning spent eating dry cereal out of the box and moping around the apartment, taking in some art didn't seem like such a bad idea. After all, it wasn't like she had any other exciting options . . .

The second—and most important reason—was that Nanna's apartment had been infiltrated by a gaggle of bloodthirsty old bats who probably were, at this very moment, gambling like a pack of drunken sailors on a twenty-four-hour shore leave.

From the moment Nanna's weekly bridge game with "the girls" began, Casey knew that she needed to flee the scene ASAP. "The girls" weren't exactly girls at all—but a decidedly unruly group of blue-haired old ladies who promptly took over the apartment with the force of a tsunami—and were, unfortunately, all about brewing endless pots of tea, munching on chocolate chip cookies from Dean & DeLuca, and asking a ridiculous number of embarrassing questions.

"Do you have a fella, Casey?" one frail lady asked, smacking her lips around her false teeth as she simultaneously shuffled her cards and poured tea into her mug.

"Don't be stupid," Nanna cackled. "My granddaughter is devoted to her studies. She doesn't have time for *boys*."

"She's too young anyway," another old bat yelled out, gobbling down a cookie and talking with her mouth full of crumbs and chocolate. "Just look at her. She's flat as a board!"

Casey felt her face turn red, and she wanted to grab a kitchen knife and put this crotchety curmudgeon out of her misery. She took a quick look at her chest—the old bat was right. It was hopeless. She was a flat-chested freak of nature who would probably never have a boyfriend.

"Nonsense," Nanna snapped. Nanna was wearing what she referred to as her "good luck" ensemble—a vintage Pucci shift in the orange and blue that almost matched the veins streaking her pale legs. "I won a thousand dollars in Monte Carlo in nineteen seventy while wearing this dress," she muttered distractedly, rubbing the worn sleeve before snapping back to reality. "And Casey is just petite—she takes after me, you know," she said proudly, slapping her cards down on the table and squealing in glee. "I won again!" As soon as Nanna had slipped her the twenty, Casey was in the elevator as fast as her feet could carry her, breathing a sigh of relief as the doors closed.

As Casey followed the map she'd picked up at the ticket counter, walking uphill to the third floor where the Kiki Smith show was currently being exhibited, she wished some of Nanna's luck would magically rub off on her. If only she had the chance to explain things to Drew! After the way she came on to him during French, he probably thought she was some kind of crazy, oversexed freak. What else did you call someone who went out of her way to attend an exhibition by an artist who was known for celebrating the female body . . . and all its various emissions?

Casey had learned about Kiki Smith from her mother, who blindly followed any artist that made work involving "women's issues," which, in the academic speak that Casey had learned to decipher at a young age, meant monthly cycles, babies, and all the other mystifying and possibly disgusting things women's bodies were capable of. Generally, "women's issues" were not Casey's cup of tea, but her mom had dragged her to a Kiki Smith retrospective at the Art Institute of Chicago one year and, grudgingly, Casey had found herself falling in love with the strange-looking wax figures dipping and trailing God-knows-what out of their you-know-whats. As disgusting as the sculptures had initially sounded, she found the softly gleaming works of wax and bronze incredibly beautiful. And to her mom's delight (and still to Casey's slight horror) she declared herself a fan—which had resulted in a long, uncomfortable talk about "women's issues" during the car ride back to Normal. Thank God she'd be going to the Guggenheim by herself this time. And going to an art exhibition by herself made her feel almost cool—not to mention kind of . . . adult. All she needed now was a pair of huge black sunglasses and a pretentious art school boyfriend to deconstruct the lithographs adorning the white walls for her, and she'd be just like any other slightly neurotic New Yorker taking in some culture on a Saturday afternoon . . .

As Casey turned the corner and walked into the sculpture gallery with its pristine white floors, the first thing she saw beside a pair of enormous bronze sculptures of women stretching their hands to the sky was Drew standing directly in front of the bronzed form of a crouching woman . . . with yellow string trailing out of her, umm, baby-maker. Drew was wearing a rumpled pair of A.P.C. khaki shorts that looked like he'd slept in them, and another one of his seemingly endless supply of white T-shirts. His brown hair was almost standing on end, and his jaw was covered with a layer of stubble that was way too thick to even call five o'clock shadow—more like nine o'clock shadow. Even though he'd clearly had a rough night and was definitely fighting the hot, he was still everything she'd ever wanted in a guy—and maybe a little more.

Casey's feet froze to the floor and her mind raced with possibilities. Should she walk over and talk to him? Things hadn't exactly went well the last time they'd hung out—if you could call a ten-minute conversation in the middle of a psychotic

French class hanging out . . . And the room was big, but it wasn't that big. There was no way she could pretend that he wasn't there. In fact, there was no way she was going to be able to walk by without him—

Drew looked up, his bloodshot blue eyes locking with hers. *Oh crap*, Casey thought smiling hopefully. *There's no backing out now*. Her face felt like it was covered with glue. Smiling was almost painful when you felt like your face might just crack off at any moment from sheer anxiety. Casey willed her feet to move and walked over, positioning herself directly in front of the sculpture.

"Hey," Drew said, turning to her and smiling. Was it her imagination, or did he not only look surprised, but almost happy to see her? "What are you doing here?"

"Oh, you know," she said, pretending to examine the sculpture and bending down to inspect the yellow rope trailing out of it. "Just checking out the show." Casey stood up and turned back to Drew. *Be cool!* her inner dating Nazi screamed, *and don't blow it this time!* "So," Casey said, trying to look like she ran into guys she was massively crushing on every day, "what do you think she's trying to *say* here?" *I really have to learn that raised eyebrow trick Madison does all the time*, Casey thought as Drew thoughtfully contemplated the sculpture.

"I don't know," he mused. "Maybe it's a commentary on the functionality of women's bodies."

"Hmmmm." Casey pretended to consider Drew's answer thoughtfully. Growing up with a mother who spouted pseudo-academic psychobabble every chance she got made her fairly confident that she could hold her own in the conversation. "Maybe you're right," she said slowly. "Or maybe she just had to *pee* really badly."

Drew cracked up and Casey laughed along at her own joke, smiling shyly when they stopped. The short silence was broken by an insistent buzzing sound coming from Drew's pants. *Of course his pants are buzzing,* Casey thought as he pulled his cell phone from his front pocket, *he's just that hot.* Drew checked the display, an annoyed expression crossing his face, switched the ringer off, and put the phone back in his pocket. Casey felt her stomach flip over. He wasn't taking the call! *Don't get too excited*, she told herself, *it was probably his mom or something.* Still, if he wasn't taking the call in front of her that had to mean *something*, didn't it?

"So." Drew shoved his hands into his pockets. "Did you just get here? I was actually just leaving."

"Oh," Casey said, the disappointment coursing through her. "Yeah, I just got here." Casey exhaled, doing her best to smile like she didn't care while blowing her hair—which was chronically misbehaving as usual—off her face. Just as she was about to make her probably ungraceful exit, her stomach erupted with a loud, menacing growl that practically echoed off the sterile, white museum walls. Dry cereal out of the box was definitely not much of a meal. Casey closed her eyes briefly. *Damn you, dry cereal*, she thought, opening them again, a sheepish expression on her face.

"A little hungry, are we?" Drew asked, clearly fighting a smile.

"Yeah," Casey mumbled, staring down at her pink Old Navy ballet flats. It was amazing—even if she didn't sabotage her pathetic excuse for a dating life through speaking, her body was sure to run it into the ground for her. "I haven't really eaten much today."

"Well, I was just about to get some food myself," Drew said. "But you probably want to check out the show, huh?"

Suddenly art couldn't have been *less* important.

"Umm, I could come back later or something," Casey said in what she *hoped* was a nonchalant tone. The last thing she needed was to come off too eager and blow it again.

"Okay, cool." Drew smiled and slung his messenger bag over his shoulder. "I was thinking of hitting Shake Shack for a burger."

Well, it wasn't a romantic dinner at Prive, but Casey guessed it was a start—and beggars couldn't exactly be choosers. Especially not beggars who miraculously got second chances . . .

"Sure," Casey said, pulling a hair elastic from her wrist, and shoving her hair back in a messy ponytail. "Is it close by?"

Drew smiled incredulously. "You've never heard of *Shake Shack*? They've only got the best burgers in the city! People sometimes line up for forty-five minutes for them."

Forty minutes and one sweaty cab ride later—during which all Casey could think about was the fact that her nose was probably shiny, and that she really needed to buy some serious sunglasses—they were sitting side by side on the soft grass in Madison Square Park, watching a group of little kids tied to a length of red string wander through—undoubtedly on their way to some museum or other horrifically cultural "outdoor activity." Casey stared down at the paper plate in her lap that held the biggest cheeseburger she'd ever seen, and wondered how the hell she was ever going to get her mouth around the thing without getting ketchup on her face—or God forbid in her *hair*.

Casey was a notoriously messy eater. Her dad always joked that when she was little, her parents used to wrap a bedsheet around her before they'd even *attempt* to feed her strained carrots or whatever other gross-ass concoction Barbara had whipped up in the Cuisinart. In any case, this burger was a dating disaster waiting to happen. Wait, were they actually even on a date? Casey wrinkled her brow and sucked her vanilla milkshake hard through her straw. Or was this just a getting-food-with-a-friend kind of thing? Either way, she was going to have to figure out a way to eat this burger without becoming covered in ketchup and grease, and without getting up and grabbing a knife and fork like some Park Avenue priss.

"You just kinda have to go for it," Drew said with a grin, the dimple that tortured her on his MySpace photo winking adorably. Casey had to practically sit on her hands to keep from reaching out to touch it. Drew raised his dripping cheeseburger to his mouth and took a huge bite, rolling his eyes and moaning with exaggerated pleasure.

Casey giggled and took a deep breath, pushing up the sleeves of her white, Old Navy cardigan, grabbing onto the gargantuan burger with both hands, and raising it to her lips.

She opened her mouth as wide as she could, and bit down into a heavenly mix of ground beef, tomatoes, and pickles, chewing like she was a contestant in a competitive eating contest.

"It's good, right?" Drew said, putting his half-eaten burger down on his plate and wiping his lips with one of the paper napkins.

"Mmmhmm." Casey nodded furiously, her mouth stuffed with cow. And, actually, it was just about the best burger to pass her lips in all of her sixteen years. It was unbelievably juicy and phenomenal—just like Drew's lips . . . And speaking of juice, Casey froze as she felt a trickle of it running down her chin. Before she could grab for the pile of napkins and wipe her face, Drew laughed like it was no big deal, leaned over with his napkin, and blotted Casey's face carefully. Casey could feel the heat from his hand through the flimsy paper, and she swallowed hard, grabbing her shake again for another sip to wash down the half of a steer she'd just managed to ingest, and to cool off her suddenly raging lust.

"Sorry," she said, trying not to feel like a total loser who couldn't eat without spilling—which, of course, she was. "This burger is beyond awesome, but messy."

"Don't worry about it," he said, shrugging off her comment and leaning back, balling up the napkin in his hand before she had time to get really embarrassed. Drew stared off into the traffic clogging Twenty-Third Street, a wistful expression coloring his face. "When I lived downtown I used to come up here after school all the time for a cheeseburger or some frozen custard. Sometimes I kind of miss it." Casey nodded, her cheeks indented from sucking on her straw so hard—she felt almost dizzy. Was it the sugar rushing headlong through her veins, or the fact that she was breathing the same air as Drew Van Allen? Drew turned to face her, a smile playing at the corners of his lips. "It's nice to see a girl actually—" he gestured at the remains of her burger, "—you know—*eat*."

Great. Was that cryptic boyspeak for "You're a fat pig eating a burger the size of your head and I'm never going to kiss you?" Suddenly, her bare thighs protruding from her Abercrombie skirt felt enormous, and she tried to surreptitiously pull down the hem without drawing his attention to her undoubtedly pasty, bulbous legs.

"No really," he said, leaning over and touching her knee lightly with his hand. "I mean it. My dad's a chef, so food's a big deal in my house."

Drew's words barely registered. Her head spun with the same thought playing over and over in an endlessly giddy feedback loop: *Drew Van Allen's hand is on my knee!* She wanted to immortalize the patch of grass they were sitting on with a bronze plaque—and it went without saying that she was never washing her knee again. Okay, maybe she'd run a hot washcloth over it when it *got* really dirty . . . From somewhere far away Drew's voice began to seep back into her lust-addled brain, and she forced herself back to reality, smiling like she hadn't just been completely lost in outer space.

". . . and speaking of food, I've been meaning to ask you: Are you going to be able to make it to my party this Saturday? I think I told you about it last week? My dad's new restaurant is catering and I need to get an idea of how many people are going to show."

"Um, uh . . ." Casey stuttered, her body desperately trying to pump some of the blood back into her throat to jump-start her vocal chords. "Of course I'll be there. I mean, you don't even want to know what Saturdays are like at my house when my grandmother's crew of bridge buddies comes over. It's terrifying," Casey said, astonished at her ability to string enough words together to form a sentence just moments after Drew Van Allen's hand had been on her knee. Her inner dating Nazi saluted her proudly.

"Awesome," Drew said. "But don't expect too much. My parents love to put these parties together, *claiming* that they're for me or for my second cousin twice removed or for the political refugees of Micronesia, but they're just an excuse to get all their friends together who insist on telling me the same stories and cracking the same jokes every time. It can be exhausting."

"Well, I can't imagine that it's worse than the Saturday bridge game. I'm there."

"Sounds good," Drew said, glancing down at his stainless D&G watch. "Shit, I'm supposed to go meet my dad to help plan the menu for the party. Between that and this burger," Drew said, tucking the final bite between his so incredibly kissable lips, *"maybe* I'll make it through until dinner."

Casey smiled as they both stood up and Drew began to walk toward the path. "I'll see you at school—and hopefully on Saturday," he said. "Oh, and my mom says to tell everyone to dress formal/casual, whatever the hell that means."

Whatever the hell indeed.

Casey watched Drew walk away, the green-tinted sunlight filtering down through the elms to bounce off the gleaming white of his T-shirt—and she would've been happy to just watch him walk for the rest of the day. *Well,* she thought as a couple on Rollerblades whizzed by, their legs encased in matching hot pink spandex bike shorts, *he may never have called, but he finally asked me out . . . I think.* A party definitely counted as a date—she was sure of it.

Finally, she began moving toward Fifth Avenue, her feet barely touching the pavement as she played out the possible scenarios of next Saturday night in her head, picturing what she might say to Drew, and, more important, what he just might say back . . .

keep it
in the
closet

Phoebe Reynaud stood in her mother's walk-in closet, surrounded by the holy trinity of Posen, Dolce, and Prada, her feet sinking into the pearl gray carpet as she surveyed the endless selection of couture—most of it intact, with the price tags still dangling. Madeline Reynaud's closet was the size of a small studio apartment—if studio apartments resembled high-end clothing shops. The scent of cedar and lavender hung sweetly in the air, and the closet was stacked floor to ceiling with more clothes, shoes, and handbags than one person could possibly ever wear in a lifetime. And speaking of lifetimes, Phoebe's would definitely be over if Madeline caught her rummaging through her stuff again . . .

School that week had been stressful times infinity, what

with Madison and Casey circling each other warily like sharks, and the killer History test she'd had on Wednesday. Now that the weekend was finally here, all Phoebe could think about was going to Drew's party tomorrow night and blowing off some serious steam—along with her sobriety . . .

Phoebe flipped through the white satin hangers in her mother's stuffed closet, the scent of Joy—Madeline's favorite perfume—wafting through the expansive space. There was the cutest Dior sundress in white eyelet and bright yellow stripes that she knew Madeline hadn't worn and wouldn't miss. Phoebe pulled the dress out and held it up to her own body, fingering the soft fabric. Besides, she knew that her mother was, at this moment, having her feet massaged at her weekly appointment at Elizabeth Arden, and by the time Madeline walked through the front door, Phoebe would be zipped up and long gone . . .

Phoebe turned to look at the large wall devoted solely to shoes. It was weird: As meticulous as Madeline was about everything in her life, her closet was always a complete *mess*. Phoebe thought she remembered her mother bringing home a pair of Jimmy Choo canary-yellow satin sandals last week, but as she looked at the endless rows of shoes, she didn't see them. Of course, she could always wear a pair of her *own* sandals, but what fun was that? Phoebe knew that she didn't have anything that would match the dress *exactly*, and as much as she didn't want to admit it, stealing from Madeline gave her a perverse thrill. Deep down she knew that getting back at her mother by taking her clothes without permission was childish and stupid, but she just couldn't seem to stop doing it. And it wasn't like

Madeline would suddenly start treating her like a daughter instead of a rival, even if she started taking more of an interest in her own closet.

There was also something about new clothes that Phoebe needed. Going out in a dress she'd worn before made her feel exposed and vulnerable—as if everyone was talking about her. She hated that feeling more than anything—and the whispering and giggling that came with it. A new outfit was armor, a kind of social protection, and the only kinds of stares Phoebe wanted to attract were those of envy. The pressure to keep up her fashion-plate image was enormous, and sometimes, when she was especially tired, Phoebe wondered what it would be like to wear sweats when she felt like it, and not wake up two hours early every morning to blow her hair out perfectly. Not that she'd be finding out anytime soon . . .

Now where *were* those shoes? Phoebe narrowed her dark eyes, scanning the crowded shelves for the coveted footwear. A flash of bright yellow at the top caught her eye, and she smiled contentedly as she held onto the custom cedar shelves with both hands, kicking off her white Coach flip-flops and climbing up to the top, her fingers closing around the bright satin ribbons. *Mission accomplished*, she thought as her hand closed around the soft, cool satin. But just as she grabbed the shoes, her left foot slipped on the smooth shelving, and she fell backward, landing in a massive pile of Vuitton luggage with only one sandal grasped in her hand.

That's just great. Now I'll have to climb up there all over again. Phoebe rubbed her tailbone—she'd landed right on a zipper—

and pushed a suitcase out of her way. As she moved the soft canvas bag, a pile of crinkled envelopes spilled out, completely covering the floor in front of her. She picked up the envelope under her foot and turned it over. The front was blank. She opened it and pulled out a piece of folded white paper. A photograph tumbled out onto the carpet, landing faceup.

Phoebe stared down uncomprehendingly. Madeline smiled into the camera, her hair pulled back in a twist that accentuated her fine bones. Phoebe recognized the ivory Oscar de la Renta silk gown her mother wore to last year's Christmas party at the Met, but the man with the dark, close-cropped beard who held Madeline around the waist, his face half-hidden in profile, was entirely unfamiliar. There was a look in Madeline's eyes that Phoebe hadn't seen in a long, long time—happiness. And everything about the photograph—from the body language to the expression on her mother's face—told her that whoever this guy was, they were definitely more than just friends. Phoebe opened the letter, the words on the page rapidly blurring from the tears filling her eyes, her head jumbled with questions. Who had taken the picture, anyway? And how long had this been going on? Suddenly, all her parents' recent arguments began to make sense. Of course her father was angry—and why shouldn't he be? Her mother was having an *affair*. Phoebe opened the letter, her eyes scanning the page.

My Darling Madeline,
When I think it's been ten hours since I've held you in my arms, I can barely stand it. Meet me tomorrow night,

8 o'clock at the Soho Grand. I'll be waiting for you—as always.

R.

Phoebe slowly refolded the letter, placing it back in the envelope, absentmindedly smoothing out the creases with the palm of her hand. There was a rustling noise in the hallway outside the bedroom door, and Phoebe jumped up, pushing the pile of envelopes back into the suitcase as fast as she could, her heart pounding. *Crap. She's home.* As Phoebe stood up, her cheeks flushed and pink, she practically ran into Madeline, who was standing in the doorway, tapping one bright red fingernail against the door frame, her eyes narrowed into a squint.

"Hey, Mom," Phoebe said nervously, unable to keep her voice from shaking, "aren't you home kind of early?" Madeline's mouth was set in a tight smile, and her glossy red lips shone above the white cashmere TSE T-shirt that exposed her prominent collarbones. Her thin legs were draped in white silk Ralph Lauren pants that swirled as she moved.

"The *real* question, Phoebe," Madeline began, her eyes sweeping the expanse of the closet, taking in the single yellow shoe on the floor, "is what you're doing in my closet, when I've specifically asked you to stay *out?*"

"I was just leaving," Phoebe said quickly, squeezing past her mother, her nostrils filling with the scent of Serge Lutens *Un Bois Vanille.* "The Van Allens' party is tomorrow night," Phoebe said as she squeezed by, trying not to brush against Madeline's clothes with her own body. "Are you going?" Phoebe stopped in the hallway, turning back to face her mother, who now had the offending yellow sandal in one hand, and was busily shaking her head in disapproval.

"No." Madeline walked over to her vanity and sat down, staring into the mirror with a dreamy, faraway expression on her face. Was it the fading sunlight coming through the huge bay windows, or did Madeline look almost rapturous sitting there? Phoebe had seen that expression before—it was the same look that came over Casey's face whenever Drew walked by, the same look that lit up Sophie's eyes when she told Phoebe about that ridiculous townie pool boy she had wanted to hook up with this past summer. "I'm simply *exhausted,*" Madeline said languidly, running a hand slowly over one cheek, a secret smile parting her lips.

"Oh," Phoebe said, backing out of the room, her stomach suddenly queasy. "Okay. Well, see you later."

Madeline nodded, picking up a MAC eyeliner brush as she leaned into the mirror. Just as Phoebe was about to make a run for it, Madeline suddenly spoke again, her eyes holding Phoebe's with a glacial stare. "Oh, and Phoebe? Before I forget—do stay *out* of my closet from now on."

"Sure," Phoebe said, swallowing hard and walking out of the room before Madeline could say anything else. As she walked the long hallway back to her own room, Phoebe's head was swimming. She couldn't believe it—her own mother, having an affair! Wasn't she too old for this kind of stuff? And what about her father? Phoebe knew for a fact that her dad despised gossip and hated the idea that anyone might be talking about him or his family. This was not going to go over well at all.

One thing was for sure, Phoebe thought as she walked into her bedroom, closing the door firmly behind her. She was going to make it her personal mission to find out both who her mother was seeing, *and* how long it had been going on—even if it tore her family apart forever.

baby
needs a
new pair
of shoes

Casey meandered along Madison Avenue, peering into store windows, sighing in awe at the amazing white taffeta Chanel tutu-style dress hanging off the plastic, anorexic body of a mannequin in the front window of Barneys. She felt like a starving person herself—with her nose pressed up against a bakery window. Why did she have to be, well, *her*? And why did money always have to be such a problem? *Umm*, her inner mediator answered back in an infinitely reasonable tone of voice, *because you moved to one of the most expensive cities in the world, and you're attending an ultra-exclusive high school where the students all get new BMWs for their sixteenth birthdays—even though the cost of parking in New York is more outrageous than rent . . .*

Okay, you've got a point, Casey thought, bringing her ridiculously priced, four-dollar iced latte up to her lips and sipping at the cool, milky drink morosely, which just reminded her that she was broke, broke, broke. Yesterday afternoon, The Bram Clan had decided to make a pit stop at Barneys after school, and Sophie and Phoebe hadn't wasted any time talking Casey into buying the distressed pair of Seven jeans she was currently wearing. As a result, she was now almost completely tapped out. When she'd left Normal, her mother had given her what she called "enough money to last a few months," but five hundred dollars was pocket change to the crowd she currently found herself in, and Casey didn't know how she was ever going to keep up. She had to look amazing at Drew's party tomorrow night—"fall to your knees and worship" amazing— but that was never going to happen if she wore anything from her moose-infested closet.

First off, Drew had practically *seen* her whole wardrobe— and she'd only been in New York a few weeks! Casey drained her drink, sucking noisily at the straw and throwing the empty cup into a metal trash can on the corner. Maybe she could just buy a cute top and wear it with her new jeans—but it wasn't like a top in any of the stores on Madison or Fifth would be any less expensive than buying a whole *dress*. Casey stared up at the blue cloudless sky and wiped away a film of sweat and humidity from her forehead. They didn't call it the Baked Apple for nothing. Living in the Midwest had taught her to tolerate the heat, but with what it did to her hair—not to mention her constant sweating—she could never really learn to love it.

Casey turned around and faced the imposing edifice that was Barneys, watching as one well-heeled, impossibly chic woman after another walked through the doors before she reluctantly turned around and began wandering aimlessly downtown, watching as the numbers on the street signs sunk gradually lower with every step she took—along with her mood. Her phone starting buzzing insistently against her leg, and she pulled it from the pocket of her new jeans, flipping it open.

"Casey," Barbara's clipped, Anglicized vowels blared through the phone. "How are you, love?"

"Okay," Casey sighed, switching ears. It was so damn hot that her phone was already the temperature of a smoking griddle, and she'd only been on it for five seconds, tops. "I guess," she added, squinting into the sun.

"I'm on my way to what promises to be a completely *fascinating* lecture on medieval gossip, of all things, and I thought I'd give you a quick jingle before I go in."

"Great," Casey said dejectedly. What was the use of living in the most exciting city in the world if she'd never have the money to really enjoy it?

"London is so fabulous this time of year. Why, the other day I was at the National Gallery and . . ."

Casey only half-listened as her mother went on and on. Sometimes she wished more than anything that Barbara was the kind of mother that she could go to with stuff like this. Weren't dates supposed to be the kind of female bonding hooha that mothers lived for? There was probably no harm in just *asking* if she could use the credit card to maybe buy a new dress for tonight. Casey took a deep breath before interrupting Barbara's endless stream of chatter.

"So, I've been invited to a party tonight, Mom," she began carefully, "by this guy that goes to my school."

"What guy? Is this a *date*?" Barbara asked, a note of panic creeping into her voice.

"I don't know," Casey mumbled, ducking into a TCBY just to get out of the heat. "Maybe?" The cold air hit her skin like a wet blanket, and goosebumps immediately broke out on her arms. She felt like a wrung-out, damp dishrag, her thin tank sticking to her back like Velcro.

"Has Nanna met him? Who is he?" Barbara demanded. Casey took a deep breath before answering as a tiny little girl dressed from head to toe in Baby Gap spilled her cup of chocolate yogurt on the floor and began wailing loudly, as if on cue. As she listened to her mother clear her throat halfway around the world, Casey was regretting opening her own mouth in the first place. No dress was worth Barbara's own particular version of the Spanish Inquisition.

"No, Nanna hasn't met him yet," Casey said, exhaling in annoyance. "His name is Drew Van Allen—he's just this guy I go to school with. His dad's a chef and his mom's some kind of painter."

"Van Allen," her mother mused, momentarily distracted. "That sounds familiar . . ." Barbara's voice trailed off and Casey could hear the wail of sirens over the staticky transatlantic line. "Wait," she said excitedly, "you don't mean *Allegra* Van Allen?"

"I *think* so," Casey said tentatively. "Why?"

"Are you sure you're *actually* my child?" Barbara snapped. "Casey, love, she's only one of the most *important* abstract expressionists in *America*!"

"Then you should be *thrilled* that I'm going to a party at her house," Casey said dryly. The vanilla frozen yogurt looked really good. Maybe she'd get a small cup as soon as Barbara was finished blathering on in her ear. With crumbled Oreos on top. There was nothing like treating herself to a small reward for surviving yet another conversation with her mother.

"So I was wondering . . ." Casey paused, listening to the sound of her mother's breathing. "I really don't have anything to wear, and I was hoping I could use the emergency credit card to maybe get a new dress for tonight." Casey winced, closing her eyes as the line filled with silence. The quiet before the storm was never a good sign where her mother was concerned.

"What's wrong with the *myriad* of dresses you brought with you?" Barbara asked, her voice measured.

"I've worn most of them," Casey said hurriedly, "and the kids around here—"

"You have a perfectly adequate wardrobe, Casey, love. And besides—" Casey heard the squeaking sound of a door opening on the other end of the line, and then a rush of wind. "—you need to learn that people like you for what's inside— not because you play into their capitalistic vision by supplementing your already quite stunning wardrobe at every turn." Barbara's academic-speak was so *annoying*. It wasn't like she was going to save the planet or anything by *not* buying a lipstick or a new dress. Casey rolled her eyes and tried not to accidentally press the END button.

"Easy for you to say when your whole life is a college campus," Casey snapped. "And stop calling me love!"

"Sorry, love," her mother said brightly. "It can't be done. Do keep me posted though. Ta now!" There was a click on the line and then silence as her mother's voice disappeared.

Casey sighed and walked to the counter, ordering a small vanilla yogurt to go, relaxing visibly as the cool, frozen treat hit her tongue, melting in her mouth and soothing the fire in her head that trying to explain anything to Barbara always managed to produce. She should've known that trying to talk to her would be a mistake: Had she learned nothing from every conversation she'd ever had with her mother for her entire life before this moment? Casey spooned the creamy dessert into her mouth and walked to the door. The ten minutes she'd spent in the frigid air-conditioning had *almost* prepared her to face the steaming pavement again.

Just as she was about to exit TCBY, a store directly across the street made her stop in her tracks: Le Nouveau Boutique: Designer Resale & Consignment. Wait . . . did that mean it was like a thrift store for rich people? Casey's clothes-induced funk began to lift as she pushed the door open and crossed the street. Le Nouveau's display window featured a constipated-looking mannequin dressed in a nubbly black-and-white Chanel suit, a vintage pearl-handled Gucci bag in one outstretched hand. Okay, this was definitely thrifting for the smart set. Even used, there was probably no way she could afford anything inside, but it wouldn't hurt to take a look around, would it? Besides, if she had to stand out on the sidewalk much longer, she'd melt into a sticky puddle of evaporated Lancôme Miracle perfume and L'Oréal texturizing spray . . .

The inside of the store was cool and dark, and smelled vaguely like her grandmother's closet. *Rich people sure must like Chanel N° 5*, Casey thought as she flipped through the racks, too terrified of the price tags to turn them over.

"Can I help you?" a kind voice from directly behind her inquired. Casey turned around and smiled at a woman around Nanna's age, a pair of bifocals hanging around a pearl-encrusted chain around her neck, dropping onto her exquisitely tailored white skirt suit. "Vintage Givenchy," she said, winking one softly wrinkled brown eye and rubbing the lapel with one pearly polished fingernail. "I've had it for years."

"It's beautiful," Casey said truthfully. The woman smiled, exposing rows of teeth so white and perfect there was no possible way they could be real.

"Well, enough about me," she said, taking Casey by the arm. "What can I help *you* with today, dear?"

"Oh, nothing," Casey stammered, her cheeks flushing. "I was just looking around. I don't really need anything right now." As soon as the lie left her lips, Casey couldn't believe she'd said it. But acting like you had more than you needed was definitely preferable to confessing how broke you were — especially in *this* neighborhood.

"Nonsense," the woman said briskly. "For instance *this*," she said, pulling out a robin's-egg-blue silk sundress with splashes of yellow flowers on the skirt, "well, it could've been designed for you!" Casey reached out and touched the soft fabric of the dress, swooning at the feel of silk on her fingertips. It didn't even look like it had ever been worn, the fabric still crisp under her hand, the colors bright. Casey pictured herself walking into Drew's undoubtedly palatial apartment, the silk swirling around her legs. As she fondled the dress, the price tag flipped over, and Casey was shocked back to reality. Four hundred dollars! For a *used* dress? Casey didn't even want to know what it cost when it was brand-new . . . it might send her into sudden cardiac arrest.

"It's a Stella McCartney original, you know," the woman said conspiratorially. "I can't tell you who she is, of course, but the young lady who donated this particular garment comes from one of the *most* powerful families in Manhattan."

Whoop-de-do, Casey thought, removing her hand from the dress reluctantly. It really didn't matter if Tinsley Mortimer herself had worn it—there was no way she'd ever be able to come up with the four hundred dollars to pay for it.

"It's lovely," Casey said, swallowing hard, "but I really can't."

"Let's just try it on first, shall we?" The saleslady pulled Casey toward the row of dressing rooms at the back of the store, the dress thrown casually over one arm. What did these old ladies eat for breakfast, anyway? Steroids? The saleslady opened up a small cubicle with a gold key and hung the dress up on a hook screwed into the light blue walls. "Just come out when you have it on," she said brightly, "and call me if you need any help."

What the hell, Casey told herself as she pulled her blue American Apparel tank over her head, kicked off her flip-flops, and stepped out of her jeans. The dress fell over her skin like water, and she smoothed it down with her hands. *Damn you, mirrorless dressing room!* Casey told herself as she opened the door and walked over to the full-length mirror on the adjacent wall.

As she stood in front of the reflective glass, Casey had to admit that the saleslady was right—the dress fit like it was made for her. Casey turned around, looking at the back of the dress and bunching her hair in her hands to get it off of her neck. It wasn't just a good dress: It was perfect. Just like the Nanette Lepore dress Madison had bought for her, this dress made her look like someone else—someone who didn't worry about money, a girl who would probably attend the Ivy League college of her choice and wind up marrying a stockbroker. Casey frowned, twirling around so that the full skirt twirled out in a circle. Wait—did she even *want* to be that girl? As she stood there looking at herself, she couldn't help but wonder what kind of deal with the devil she was making by trying to become a member of the most popular clique in school—maybe in all of Manhattan. But the dress *was* beautiful. It made her feel a little like Cinderella on her way to the ball. *Yeah, right*, her inner cynic snorted. *Just remember: That joiner had to give the dress back at midnight—and the stupid coach turned into a pumpkin . . .*

"I was right." Casey jumped as the saleslady snuck up behind her and adjusted the thin straps along her freckled shoulders. God, she hated her freckles—it was like constantly having an incurable case of smallpox. "It's perfect on you!"

"Yeah," Casey said, surveying her reflection uneasily, "I love it, but . . ." Casey's voice trailed off as she looked at the price tag dangling from underneath her arm. "But I can't really afford it," she said, meeting the saleslady's eyes in the mirror. "I should've told you that from the start." As soon as she said it, she knew that it was true. Why was she all of a sudden pretending to be someone else? What was wrong with just being Casey Anne McCloy? There was no way she was ever going to really fit in at Meadowlark anyway—or with The Bram Clan— so why did she keep trying? She was always going to fail. And, as much as she wanted to fit in, she wasn't sure she wanted to become some kind of Stepford clone of an Upper East Side princess.

"Thanks for letting me try it on," Casey said, preparing to walk back inside the dressing room.

"Not so fast," the saleslady said, grabbing Casey by the wrist, her dark eyes shining with amusement.

"I told you, really—I can't afford it." Casey glanced down at the chipped pink polish on her fingers.

"Well, what *can* you afford?"

"I, um . . . I can't afford much at all," Casey said, her face blushing with embarrassment at having to talk about being broke with such a put-together and kind old lady—not to mention while wearing such a dress. "I'd be hard-pressed to give you a hundred bucks for it . . . and I know that's just not enough."

The saleslady smiled at her through the mirror and Casey could swear that she heard the gears in her brain cranking away. "Well, I'll tell you what, dear. I'll tell you what we'll do. Take the dress—it looks perfect on you and it would pain me to sell it to anyone else after seeing it on you. You give me fifty dollars for it now and then promise me—you have to promise—that you'll come help me sort through boxes of donations sometime in order to work off the rest." The gears ground to a halt and a new, bigger smile crawled across her barely wrinkled lips, content with having solved the problem. "So that's that!" she cried, pushing Casey back into the dressing room before she even had a chance to think about the offer, much less muster any sort of reply. "We'll wrap that beauty up and you'll be on your way."

Although there was no mirror in the dressing room, Casey imagined that if she could see herself or if anyone were watching her, it would seem that, by slipping off the dress, she was becoming someone entirely different—a freckled, frizzed-out tourist from Nowhere, Illinois—a person that she wasn't sure she wanted to leave behind entirely.

It's just a dress, she reminded herself. *And an awesome one at that*. She stepped into her plain-old outfit, threw the dress over one shoulder, and walked out toward the register, certain that she—Casey Anne McCloy—was going to look fantabulous at Drew's party.

meet
the
parents

✧

Drew leaned his elbows on the butcher-block top of the island that dominated the Van Allen kitchen, watching as his dad's hands moved deftly around a ten-inch Wüsthof chef's knife, reducing a pile of raw carrots to expertly cut cubes. Drew smiled, taking a sip of his Kir Royale as he watched his dad work, his hands a blur. It was so totally predictable. Even though his dad's new Cajun-fusion restaurant was doing most of the catering, Drew knew that his father would never be one of those guys who left the kitchen drudgery to someone else. He was always sneaking in to rearrange piles of green, leafy salads, cutting perfectly executed garnishes with a paring knife, and helping the catering team dice huge bundles of root vegetables.

"So, are you excited about tonight?" His dad arranged a platter of baby lamb chops around a puddle of fragrant sauce on a bed of baby lentils, so that the entire plate resembled a bunch of flowers in bloom—or a gunshot wound, depending on how you looked at it.

"Uh, yeah." Drew rolled his eyes, taking another gulp of his Kir as the champagne bubbles tickled his nose, making him sneeze. He'd gotten hooked on the combination of champagne and black-currant liquor during a champagne-and-chocolate-croissant-soaked week in Paris this past summer. "I can barely contain myself."

His dad pushed the finished platter to the side and looked Drew in the eye, his gaze deadly serious.

"Do I detect a note of sarcasm, Master Van Allen?"

"Very perceptive," Drew answered, leaning over and topping off his glass with the cool, open bottle of Dom on the countertop.

"I'm *sorry*." Drew's dad cupped his ear with one hand and tilted his head, gesturing to the men working behind him who were stirring bubbling pots, and dicing onions. "Did you guys *hear* something?" His dad waved the chef's knife around in Drew's general direction, slicing the air and grinning maniacally. The caterers shook their heads, trying not to laugh.

"That's hilarious, Dad," Drew deadpanned, crossing his arms over his chest. "I'm *shaking* with laughter."

"Seriously, Drew." His dad poured himself a glass of champagne, draining it in one gulp and wiping his salt-and-pepper beard with the back of his hand. "Isn't there *anything* about tonight that you're even remotely excited about?" His dad motioned to the platters of hors d'oeuvres covering every available surface in the kitchen. "Or has all of this hard work been for nothing? You do realize that I'm wasting my *golden* years *slaving* away in the kitchen for your benefit, don't you?"

Drew shrugged his shoulders and finished his champagne. "Nice try, Dad—you're barely in your forties. Since when does that constitute your *golden* years?"

"I could go at any time!" his dad yelled out gleefully, twirling his chef's knife in one hand, and attacking a bunch of spinach. "Aren't the Macallisters coming tonight?"

"Don't remind me," Drew mumbled, popping a piece of prosciutto-wrapped melon into his mouth and chewing loudly.

"What? Are you and Madison on the outs again? You just got back in town!"

"I know," Drew said morosely, swallowing the hunk of melon, which stuck like a lump in his chest. "That's what makes it so tragic."

Drew's dad smiled, the spinach reduced to neat, finely shredded piles. "You know, Drew, you come from a *very* artistic family."

"No, *really*, Dad?" Drew widened his eyes in feigned astonishment. "You can't be serious."

"As a heart attack." His dad brought the cutting board over to the sink and swept it clean with a damp rag. "Madison *is* gorgeous," he mused turning on the garbage disposal, which promptly ate the collection of vegetable scraps like a hungry mechanical monster.

"Don't remind me," Drew answered while rolling up the sleeves of his white Gucci dress shirt.

"But she's a little . . . boring," his dad said thoughtfully.

"Then it's a good thing *you* don't have to date her," Drew snapped.

"Maybe you need someone a little more . . . *challenging*."

"Trust me, Dad—Madison's *plenty* challenging."

His dad turned around, wiping his hands on the clean chef's towel he always kept draped over his left shoulder. Except tonight it looked completely ridiculous, considering that he was wearing gray Paul Smith dress pants in a slightly textured wool, and a black dress shirt he'd had custom-made on their family trip to London last spring.

"I meant *mentally*, Drew." His dad threw the towel back over his shoulder and crossed his arms over his chest. "Maybe she's just not creative enough for you."

Drew walked over to the fridge and got out another bottle of Dom, staring at the condensation on the green bottle as if the tiny droplets of water could somehow tell him what to do next. Maybe his dad was right—as much as he was attracted to Madison, maybe the only thing they really had in common at the end of the day was the fact that they were the couple that was most likely to couple. It wasn't like they routinely sat around sharing their deepest feelings with one another, or engaging in heated debates about the upcoming presidential race. When he first moved uptown, the only thing that had made him feel like he even remotely fit in anywhere anymore was his relationship with Madison. Before that, every spare moment was spent downtown with his old friends—he wanted nothing to do with the people he saw every day at Meadlowlark. But the girls were another story . . . and that, he could see now, was where this whole mess had begun. For a while, knowing that he was dating the most gorgeous girl in school, the girl every other guy in Manhattan dreamed about nightly, had been enough. Now, he just didn't care.

Besides, dating Madison made him feel like a character in some awful teen movie where everyone had perfect smiles and exceedingly shiny hair, got in to the Ivy league school of their choice without so much as breaking a sweat—stepping all over everyone else in their pointy stiletto heels in the process. There was no denying it—Madison had been a huge part of his life during the past two years, and he still really couldn't imagine his day-to-day existence without her in it in some way. But that was the past. And try as he might, Drew couldn't seem to block out that little voice inside his head that told him that Casey just might be his future. But if this thing with him and Casey was going to happen, he was definitely going to take it slow this time—if he'd learned anything from his experience dating the emotional tsunami that was Madison Macallister, it was not to rush into a relationship—or whatever it was they'd been to one another—so fucking fast. *And one date does not a relationship make,* he reminded himself as the doorbell sounded, shattering his thoughts.

Drew's dad looked down at the gleaming mother-of-pearl face of his Cartier Panther watch, his forehead wrinkling into a frown. "Whoever it is," he said dryly, "they're *extremely* early."

Drew heard the sound of his mother's voice in the hallway, high-pitched and welcoming, and then the tap-tap of heels as the first annoyingly overpunctual guest approached the kitchen door. Casey walked into the bustling room wearing a sheepish expression and a blue dress splashed with yellow flowers that made her mass of curly golden hair shine in the light. Her legs extended long and bare from the silky fabric, and her face was brushed with just a dusting of powder so that her freckles showed through. All at once, Drew was filled with the impulse to pull her to him and lick the small brown dots that peppered her cheeks and nose—just to see if they were as cinnamon-sweet as they looked. Drew felt his breath catch in his throat as he stared at her, unable to pull his eyes away.

"Hey," she said nervously, her cheeks reddening. "I guess I'm a little *too* early."

"Nonsense!" Drew's dad bellowed, pouring Casey a glass of champagne and adding the barest drop of black-currant liquor. "Being fashionably early is the new pork belly!"

Drew rolled his eyes at Casey. "Dad, what did we tell you about restaurant-speak in social settings?"

"That it doesn't work?"

"Exactly." Drew rolled his eyes at Casey, who smiled back tentatively. Why had he never realized how *pretty* she was before? He'd thought she was cute in that yellow thing she had on the other day, but now, in the blue silky dress she had on, which left her shoulders bare, she looked totally stunning. Drew peered at the dress closely. There was something about it that looked scarily familiar to him, jogging his memory. It was almost like he remembered it from somewhere. *Whatever*, Drew shrugged, pushing the thought to the back of his mind, *I probably saw it in one of Mad's stupid fashion magazines*. Drew grabbed the Kir from his father, handing it over to Casey—who immediately began warily eyeing the bubbly, slightly pink concoction.

"It's a Kir," Drew explained, holding up his own glass and taking a sip to show his solidarity. "I got scarily addicted to them in Paris this past summer."

Casey raised the glass to her lips and closed her eyes as she swallowed. "It's good!" she said with equal parts surprise and excitement, opening her eyes widely this time. "I don't usually like the taste of alcohol," she said apologetically to Drew's dad.

"Me neither," Drew's dad said with a chuckle as he poured himself another drink.

"I'm sure you've probably figured this out already," Drew said to Casey while placing his glass down on the countertop and pointing to his father, "but this is my dad, Robert Van Allen."

"I'm Casey McCloy." Casey held out her hand and shook his dad's hand with a firm grip, a determined expression on her face. Even though some people might think it was a little corny, Drew actually really liked the fact that she obviously wanted to make a good impression on his parents. She was the complete polar opposite of Madison, who avoided his parents—and parents in general—at all costs.

"Pleased to meet you, Casey," his dad said, holding out a platter of pea pod–wrapped shrimp to Casey and watching as she took a bite, her eyes widening with pleasure. "Though I have to say—if you're hanging out with this one," he motioned to Drew with a jutting thumb, "you might want to think about having your head examined," he added smugly, popping a melon ball into his mouth.

"Some people in this nuthouse are definitely in need of psychiatric attention," Allegra Van Allen said as she entered the room in a flowing, white Grecian gown, her hair pulled back in a dark twist shot through with metallic gold cord in an intricate geometric pattern, "but I doubt our son is one of them." Drew watched with a mixture of pride and embarrassment as his mom walked over and linked her arm through his father's, staring up into his face with wide, dark eyes, a smile turning up the edges of her rose-colored lips.

"You are an absolute goddess." Drew smiled at Casey as they watched his father lean down and whisper into his mother's ear. "Did I mention that I love you in unreasonable amounts?" he went on playfully as he bent even lower, biting her neck. Allegra rolled her eyes helplessly at Drew and Casey, then swatted her husband away with feigned exasperation and short, red-varnished fingernails.

"Stop being such a *pest*," she said with a half-smile, reaching one hand up and smoothing her hair. She turned to Casey, placing one hand on Casey's bare arm. "Don't get married," she whispered conspiratorially, "they become pests overnight when you marry them."

Casey grinned. "I'll try to remember that. By the way, my mom wanted me to tell you that she's a huge fan of your work—and I can see why. Your paintings are gorgeous."

"I like this one, Drew." Allegra nodded her head approvingly, the gold shadow on her eyelids gleaming in the light. "Smart *and* beautiful."

"A keeper," his dad called out as he handed the first silver trays to the waiters lined up at the kitchen door.

"Oh my God," Drew said laughingly, "we have to get out of here—or they'll keep this up all night."

"Why don't you show her the view from the terrace," his mother suggested with a wink. "The setting sun over the tops of the buildings is really . . ." His mother's voice broke off as she stared dreamily at his father, who put down the tray he was holding and walked over, clasping her to his side.

"Romantic," his father finished, taking his mother's hand between his own and bringing it up to his lips.

"Okay, we're out of here," Drew said briskly, grabbing Casey's hand. "Before I throw up."

"Can we go check out the terrace?" Casey asked excitedly, her voice a low whisper. Drew looked over at her happy, glowing face. Another thing he was really beginning to like about Casey was the way everything was so new to her. She was capable of finding pleasure and surprise in something as small as a cheeseburger—or a terrace.

"Of course," Drew said confidently as he led Casey through the living room, where waiters in tuxedos were beginning to set up the long table filled with food, and out onto the terrace, where the last streaks of purple, yellow, and pink lit up the rapidly darkening sky.

strangers
in the
night

Phoebe walked into the Van Allens' apartment with Sophie trailing close behind her, craning her neck to search for Madison over the crush of bodies. The room glowed softly from the ivory candles in sparkling cut-crystal holders that dominated every available surface. Who *were* these people anyway? she wondered, looking over the mostly unfamiliar sea of faces. Through the large, floor-to-ceiling windows in the Van Allens' living room, Phoebe could see delicate strings of white Japanese lanterns illuminating the terrace. A pyramid of champagne glasses dominated the long buffet table set up in front of the windows, golden liquid frothing and bubbling around the thin crystal glasses.

"I don't see Mad anywhere." Sophie scanned the well-dressed

crowd, her green eyes flitting back and forth like luminous, fighting fish. Phoebe snorted, dismissing Sophie's ridiculous comment. If years of experience had taught them both anything about Madison, it was that she made it a point to be chronically late. Even if she *were* there, she'd no doubt be holding court in the center of the room, guys buzzing around her like bees pollinating a rose. She wouldn't exactly be hiding in a corner. In fact, she'd probably be getting totally random guys to fetch her blinis from the buffet table, or a Diet Coke from the bodega down the street.

Not that Phoebe was jealous or anything. She knew that she was pretty, but she also knew that she didn't have Madison's seemingly bottomless self-confidence. Whenever guys talked to her, she felt decidedly stupid. She never knew what to do or say—or even how to act. And even though she'd spent years watching Madison wrap Drew—and everyone else in the near vicinity—around her little finger, Phoebe didn't feel like she'd made much progress on the dating front. Whenever a cute guy came up and talked to her, Phoebe always felt like her mouth was glued shut with peanut butter. It was completely annoying—not to mention embarrassing.

"Wow," Sophie whispered behind her as she took in the candlelit room and the murmuring hum of the crowd. "Maybe we can meet some cute artist guys or something."

"Right," Phoebe said sourly. "Use your eyes—they're all, like, *thirty*!"

"So what?" Sophie smiled, pushing her bangs away from her left eye with exaggerated movements while simultaneously

admiring her candy-pink Tocca mini dress. "I could be down
with dating an older guy."

"Uh-huh." Phoebe rolled her eyes and played nervously
with the leather fringes on her cream-colored Balenciaga mo-
torcycle bag. "And can you imagine your mom's reaction when
she found out?"

"She doesn't have much room to criticize *my* actions right
now," Sophie answered cryptically, as her usually open, rosy
face darkened. "Ugh, I really have to pee," she said crankily.
"And I always forget where the bathrooms are here. Drew's
apartment is like an art-infested labyrinth of pretension where
all the toilets are 'installations' or something."

"True." Phoebe sighed as they pushed their way into the
room. "I think there's definitely one over *there*," she said,
pointing to the hallway leading to the kitchen and beyond.

"Okay," Sophie said with a smile, her skin glowing with
Guerlain's Terracotta bronzing powder. "I'll be back in a sec.
Meet me by the food?" Phoebe nodded, smoothing down her
white Ralph Lauren sheath with sweaty palms. Why did she
always get so nervous at parties? It wasn't likely that this one
would be any different than the million other stupid Upper
East Side soirees she'd been forced to attend since she was
in diapers.

Phoebe stood in front of the buffet table, pretending to
contemplate a silver platter of toast points piled with Beluga
caviar and crème fraîche, awkwardly crossing her arms over her
chest and simultaneously praying that someone she knew—
anyone—would come up to talk to her. The artfully arranged

platters of food smelled delicious, but over the years she'd made it a rule to never eat at these things. The last thing she needed was to get stuck in a conversation with some totally yummy random guy with a dripping toast point in one hand and a glass of champagne in the other. A mouthful of fish eggs was definitely the anticute. And speaking of cute, the hottest guy she'd ever seen was looking right *at* her.

He was standing a few feet away, his blue eyes boring into her white dress like he had X-ray vision. She hoped for her sake that he didn't—otherwise he'd not only know that she was wearing an ivory lace bra and thong set from La Perla, but he'd also know just how cute she thought he was. His tanned arms hung loosely from a crisp white dress shirt, which he wore untucked over dirty-washed A.P.C. jeans. A bright blue silk tie hung loosely around his neck, and dark, silky hair hung down into his startlingly blue eyes. His full, red lips curled into a smile as her gaze met his. Phoebe nervously looked down at her silver Dior sandals, trying to keep her heart from beating its way out of her chest. When she looked up, he was standing right in front of her, grinning widely.

"Hey," he said, his eyes locked on her face. "Now that we're face-to-face, I can see that it's a good thing I came over," he answered, smiling confidently. He reached over and picked up a toast point from the platter on the table, popping the whole thing in his mouth. It was amazing how cute guys were always so totally un-self-conscious—they ate like pigs in front of girls and never even thought twice about it. As he leaned in, Phoebe practically swooned. He smelled like a tropical beach on a hot day. His body gave off the enticing aroma of citrusy cologne mixed with something salty-sweet—and completely delicious.

"Why is that?" Phoebe asked nervously.

He swallowed the mouthful of caviar and toast, and grabbed another off the tray. "Well, you're *much* too pretty to be standing here all by yourself."

Phoebe smiled, biting her bottom lip to keep from collapsing into a pile of nervous giggles. The cutest guy she'd ever seen was totally flirting with her—and she didn't have the faintest idea of what to do or say next. Life was totally unfair. Phoebe got almost as much male attention as Madison, but the difference was that Phoebe seemed to always end up blowing it by laughing or saying something stupid at the most crucial moment . . .

"Are you a friend of Drew's?" Phoebe asked, looking away from the intensity of his gaze.

"Sort of," he said, popping the toast point into his mouth. "Actually, he's more my sister's friend than mine." If she could've had a direct conversation with God, she would've asked him to create this guy. He was practically redefining the definition of hot with every passing moment.

"So why are you here then?" Phoebe asked, reaching over and grabbing a glass of champagne to play with. At least she'd have something in her hands to distract her from the fact that she wanted to kiss this guy—whoever he was—more than she'd ever wanted to kiss anyone in her entire life.

"For the free gourmet snacks, of course." He shoved his hands in his front pockets, grinning widely. "And the pretty girls," he added, looking her slowly up and down. *Okay,* Phoebe thought, inhaling deeply, *this guy is definitely trouble.* He probably consumed girls like her the way he ate toast points—daily. Wait, check that—maybe *hourly.* She was in completely over her head and way out of her league. Looking into his eyes—the blue of the Caribbean—she thought, inexplicably, about her mother. If the adrenaline rush she was feeling right now was anything like what her mother experienced each time she met her "friend"—or *whatever* he was—Phoebe was beginning to see why deviating from the sanctity of marriage might be more than just a little compelling, not to mention dangerous.

"You don't remember me, do you?" the boy said, a smile curling up at the edges of his all-too-kissable lips, and then under his breath, almost to himself, he mumbled, "and maybe that's a good thing . . ."

"Where would I remember you from? I don't *know* you, do I?" Pheobe said, hoping that she wasn't in the midst of some massive faux pas that would result in her losing any chance at even five minutes with this guy in an *extremely* dark room. But how on earth could she possibly forget someone like him? "Do I know your sister or something?"

The guy's seemingly unbreakable cool cracked just slightly at her question, a cloud passing quickly over his eyes, his hands grabbing at another toast point to jam into his maw in an attempt to cover his uneasiness. Phoebe was thrown off by this complete one-eighty. Had she done something wrong? Said something wrong? *I didn't even move,* she thought, again feeling perplexed, wondering how she could salvage a conversation that was proving to be more confusing than an episode of *Lost*. *He looks exactly how I feel*, Phoebe thought, wondering just what the hell was going on.

"Um, you've probably seen her around, you know . . . I mean, everyone kind of knows everyone up here, right?"

"Well, what's her name?" she asked, wanting more than ever to get to the bottom of this. The guy shifted his weight from right foot to left, his face coloring deeply as he looked at her, unable—or unwilling—to speak.

"There you are!" Sophie proclaimed as she broke the awkward silence between them and walked up to Phoebe, regarding the guy—who Phoebe had silently nicknamed Total Hotness—with obvious disdain. "What are you *doing* here?" she asked, her tone radiating utter dislike. "Isn't it bad enough I have to *live* with you without you showing up here and molesting my friends, too?"

Sophie turned to Phoebe, a fierce expression taking over her usually placid features. "Was he bothering you?" she demanded, her hands on her hips. Phoebe opened her mouth to protest, but just as she was about to speak, Sophie waved her hand dismissively, cutting her off. "Don't answer that," she added, the diamond studs in her ears glinting in the candlelight. "Of *course* he's bothering you—he's my brother, he can't help it."

"Oh, so *now* I'm your brother?" the guy asked with a mischievous smile. Phoebe felt like her brain had been washed in battery acid. This gorgeous guy was Sophie's brother? The

219

last time she'd seen Jared was two Christmases ago when he'd organized some ridiculous lacrosse game in the St. John family room with a bunch of sweaty boys in boxers and plaid knee socks—and she'd been decidedly unimpressed.

"Okay, okay," he said, smiling sheepishly. "I guess the cat's out of the bag."

"What are you *talking* about?" Sophie asked irritably.

"I'm Jared," the guy formerly known as Total Hotness said, holding out his hand. Phoebe grabbed on in a state of shock, moving her wrist up and down in a daze. "Sophie's brother."

"Ugh, you are *not* my brother, so just get over it," Sophie snapped, rolling her eyes.

"Whoa—chill out, bra," Jared said soothingly, placing one hand on his sister's shoulder—a hand that Sophie shrugged off immediately.

"Stop calling me bra!" Sophie grabbed a glass of champagne and downed it in one long swallow. "I don't even know what that *means*. And why are you introducing yourself to Phoebe anyway. I've only known her since I was two."

"I didn't recognize him," Phoebe said in what she hoped was a placating voice. She felt like she was walking on eggshells—or land mines. She'd never seen Sophie this cranky. She'd never even seen her *angry*. Sophie generally had the ecstatically happy, slightly crazed disposition of a game show host. "He's been gone for a long time, Soph."

"Not long enough," Sophie snorted, grabbing another glass of champagne, sipping more slowly this time. Sophie grabbed Phoebe by the hand and pulled her toward the terrace before she could say good-bye, before she could even speak. As they reached the large French doors, Sophie turned around to face Phoebe, a strange expression on her face.

"You don't . . . like him or anything, do you, Pheebs?" There was almost a pleading note in Sophie's voice, and all at once Phoebe felt terrible, like she'd been flirting with someone else's boyfriend—or brother.

"What do you mean?" Phoebe asked nervously, playing with the leather fringes on her bag. "Of course not." Sophie's face relaxed into a smile, and she squeezed Phoebe's hand, momentarily reassured. Phoebe got a sinking feeling in her stomach. As soon as the words had left her lips, she knew they were a lie.

"Come on," Sophie said happily, pushing her bangs from her eyes. "Let's go outside. I think I see Casey." Phoebe allowed Sophie to lead her out the door, but she couldn't help turning back one last time to look at Jared, who stood right where she'd left him. As she looked back at his beautiful face, he winked, and a spark of electricity went through her as the blood rushed to her face.

Call me, he mouthed, bringing his index finger and thumb up to his mouth in a pantomime of a telephone receiver. Phoebe shook her head from side to side, mouthing back *no way*, before she turned back to Sophie and walked out onto the darkening terrace, the stars peeking out of the sky in quick flashes of white light.

green-eyed monster

Madison stepped into the front hall of the Van Allen apartment as one of the caterers assigned to door-duty took her lightweight, hot pink pashmina wrap from her shoulders. It was nine P.M., and she was officially one hour late—and that meant that it was just about time to make her grand entrance. If Edie had ever taught her anything even *remotely* useful, it was that being fashionably late was a must. And she had to admit that she absolutely loved it when the room stopped and all eyes turned to stare at her. So she was an attention whore, so what? There were worse things you could be—like totally, irredeemably unfashionable, which she most certainly was *not*. Madison looked down at her black satin Armani sheath dress, the rhinestone buckles on her new black Manolos glinting in the light. She paused ever-so-slightly, her heart fluttering in anticipation of the sea of eyes that would be trained on her when she looked up. She walked out through the foyer—a slight catwalk swing in her hips—but was greeted by nothing more than a low hum of voices and clicking crystal. *Fuckers*, Mad thought to herself, walking normally now, her shoulders slightly slouched, *they better not have eaten all of the salmon pâté, too, or I'm really going to be pissed*.

Every time Madison stepped into the Van Allens' opulent prewar apartment, she felt almost dizzy. Huge, brightly colored paintings that resembled the drawings Bijoux made in art class shrieked at her from every available expanse of wall space. *Maybe I really just don't understand art*, Madison thought as she stepped into the spacious but crowded living room, *but these painting are beyond atrocious*. And Madison was no stranger to atrocious lately, it seemed. Ever since Drew had left her standing there in front of The Bram like an idiot, she'd wondered what exactly she'd say when she saw him tonight. She was furious, that went without saying, but more than anything, she was completely confused. How could he just walk away when she'd been so, umm . . . *welcoming*? Okay, so she really meant *easy*, but still. She'd been ready to give the whole physical side of their relationship a second chance, and he'd just shrugged and walked away! Not that she was totally surprised. Drew had been acting all kinds of weird since he got back from Europe (Okay, so he wasn't exactly normal *before* he left either), and she couldn't help wondering just how much of his strangeness was due to the presence of a certain curly-haired stranger . . .

But tonight she intended to find out. As soon as she saw Drew, she would definitely corner him and get some kind of an explanation out of him—one way or another. And if Casey got in her way, she was going *down*. It was really that simple. She'd had just about enough of the wide-eyed innocent act everyone else at Meadowlark, including Drew, seemed to fall for.

Madison squared her shoulders like she was preparing for battle, and scoped out the terrain. The vast room was filled to the max—women in Prada dresses and men in suits or tuxedos pushed up against the brightly colored walls. Mad hated the feeling of squeezing into a room—and the huge bouquets of field flowers and lilies that dominated every surface didn't help her feel any less claustrophobic either. A few pretentious art snobs with total assitude prowled the room in their all-black ensembles, complete with paint smears (at least she *hoped* it was paint) on their tight, black pants. *Eeew*. Madison shuddered delicately. It looked like the entire population of Williamsburg had thrown up most of its inhabitants directly onto the turquoise-and-white op art carpets of the Van Allens' living room. Maybe they'd all have an unprovoked art-attack en masse, and scurry back to their dingy studios like cockroaches. And why did artists always have to be so gross and unwashed?

She sighed with annoyance as she scanned the room looking for Drew, Phoebe, or Sophie, who were, of course, nowhere to be found. For lack of anything better to do, Madison walked over to a long, white-draped table filled with delicious-smelling appetizers, and popped a piece of bacon-wrapped shrimp in her mouth as she looked out the sliding glass windows to the Van

Allens' terrace—which was, unfortunately, just as crowded as the apartment. As she chewed the delicious, salty, bacony goodness, Madison caught sight of a mop of yellow hair at the far corner of the terrace, and pushed slowly through the crowd to get a better look. And what she saw made her swallow hard— then completely lose her appetite.

Drew and Casey stood close together on the terrace as the last streaks of light faded from the sky. She watched through the glass in horror as Drew reached up and tenderly pushed a stray curl from Casey's face, stopping to caress her cheek with his index finger, smiling softly. Oh. No. She. Didn't! Madison felt her blood begin to churn as the little green monster inside of her rapidly expanded to Incredible Hulklike proportions. In fact, her little green monster made the Jolly Green Giant look like a total pussy. And WTF? Why the hell was Casey wearing the dress she'd given Edie to donate to charity two months ago? She'd know that dress *anywhere*. It was a one-of-a-kind, for starters, and the hem in the back was coming down slightly from where she'd caught it on a chair at some stupid benefit Edie had dragged her to at the Met last spring. Not that anyone would ever notice the slight tear but her. *Well*, she thought smugly, *she certainly is a charity case all right. And if the dress fits* . . .

Madison opened the terrace door and walked out into the humid evening air, just as Drew put both hands on Casey's shoulders, leaning in to whisper into her ear. *That's about enough* of that, Madison thought, her sandals clicking confidently on the Italian marble tiles that Drew's crazy mom had shipped over from Florence. She stopped right in front of their oblivious faces, staring at each other with lust-crazed eyes that made her want to hurl up her undigested shrimp at their feet in a fishy-smelling puddle.

"Well," she said, her lips, painted with MAC Lacquer in Fanplastico, curling into a sneer. "Don't you two look *cozy*."

At the sound of her voice, Casey and Drew jumped apart like they'd been struck by lightning. *In a minute, they're going to wish they had been*, Madison thought with no small degree of satisfaction as she took in the panicked expression on Casey's face. Better to be feared than loved—that was for sure. It gave you so much more—what was the word? Ah, that's right—leverage. Madison crossed her arms over the sleek fabric of her dress. It was weird how close crying and complete and utter rage really were at the end of the day. If she wasn't so angry right now she knew that she'd probably start blubbering away like an idiot. It wasn't fair. People in her life just kept disappearing—first her father and now Drew.

"Madison," Casey's voice shook slightly as she spoke. "We weren't sure you were coming."

"Oh, I wouldn't miss it for the world," Madison said airily, looking Casey over with a practiced eye. "But tell me," she said, moving closer, reaching out to grasp the material of the dress in her fingertips. "Wher*ever* did you find my old dress? Have you been playing in the *garbage*?" Madison turned to Drew, her green eyes cool and impassive.

"You see, I gave that dress to my mother to donate to *charity* two months ago," Madison sneered, relishing Casey's obvious embarrassment as she turned bright red, then looked at the floor, unable to meet Madison's gaze. "Come to think of it," Madison went on, placing one perfectly manicured finger against her chin, "it seems like ever since you moved here you've been interested in *everything* that belongs to me, haven't you?"

Madison watched with satisfaction as Casey looked up, opening her unglossed lips, and then rapidly closing them. *She looks like a fucking guppy*, Madison thought triumphantly. *And what would Drew want with a loser fish who can't dress and has incredibly unfortunate hair—when he could have* me? She smiled smugly, her eyes like frozen jade chips as she reached over and twined her arms around Drew's neck, pulling him close. Drew's face was a mass of confusion as she wrapped her body around his, pulling his face down for a kiss as her tongue snaked into his mouth. At first his lips were tense and hard as they touched hers, but as she held on she felt his body give way and melt into hers. And before she knew it, he was opening his mouth and kissing her back. Madison opened her eyes and stared at Casey, who had gone suddenly white, as if a vampire had swooped down onto the terrace while their eyes were closed and drained her of all her blood. *Serves you right,* Madison gloated as she closed her eyes again. *You messed with the wrong girl . . .*

"I'm so sorry I'm late, baby," she purred when they broke apart, reaching up and smoothing Drew's hair back with her fingers. "But I'm here *now*."

"I should . . ." Casey stammered, her eyes darting wildly from Drew to Madison, then back again. "I should . . ."

"Go?" Madison deadpanned, one arched eyebrow raised, her lips curled into a smirk. "Good idea."

"I'll go," Casey said, her voice shaking slightly, "but I want you to know something first. Ever since I moved here, I just wanted to be your friend—I didn't *plan* . . . this." She gestured at the space between herself and Drew with one hand. "It just *happened*."

"Nothing *'just happens,'*" Madison answered back, her green eyes like slits. "Everyone here has an agenda—even *you*."

"If that's true," Casey said, a tear spilling from her right eye and sliding down her cheek, "then I guess you do, too." Before Madison could respond, Casey turned and walked quickly back toward the Van Allens' apartment, tripping on Sophie's wedge heels and the slickly tiled patio, twisting her ankle and falling to the ground. Madison giggled, rolling her eyes as she watched Casey pick herself back up, blood running down her leg from a skinned knee before she ran inside, fumbling with the huge sliding doors. Madison turned back to Drew, smiling expectantly. Thank God she'd come along and saved Drew from the hell of trying to date some uncoordinated, totally spastic freak who couldn't even run *away* without falling. *Whatever*, Madison thought as she reached over and took Drew's hand, *I'm sure he'll think of a way to thank me later* . . .

"Now," she purred, her green eyes flashing. "Where were we?"

the
big
blowout

"What the hell are you *doing*, Mad?" Drew pushed Madison away, stepping back and crossing his arms over his chest. His face felt strange and tight with an uncomfortable mix of confusion and fury. The look on Casey's open, freckled face as she ran away played itself out over and over in his brain until he thought he might lose it completely.

"What am *I* doing?" Madison snarled, tossing her silky platinum hair from her shoulders. "What are *you* doing, Drew? You ask me out the other night, and then you freak out at my door and run *away*, and the next thing I know you're here with that *girl*."

"Her name is *Casey*." Drew ran his hands through his hair

and began to pace the way he always did when he was mad or freaked-out—or both. He couldn't remember the last time he was this angry, and if he'd ever been this completely furious at Madison specifically, he'd blocked it out. But deep inside he wondered if just maybe he was maddest at himself. There was no way he should've responded when Mad kissed him, but when it came to Madison, his body seemed to have a life—and mind—of its own.

"And you just treated her like crap, you know that, Mad? She didn't deserve that!"

"Oh, poor baby." Madison pursed her lips out into the full-lipped pout that usually drove him half-crazed with lust, her voice dripping with fake sympathy. "My heart really bleeds for her."

"We were just talking!" Drew shouted, throwing his arms in the air. All at once the crowded terrace fell silent, the party-goers staring at Drew and Madison surreptitiously over their half-full glasses. The Upper East Side was a very small world—a microcosm really, and Drew knew that by Monday, the fight he was currently having in front of practically everyone he knew would be all over polite society. As it was, Dominique Delmonico, the biggest gossip on the Upper East Side—if not all of Manhattan—was standing less than ten feet away, peering at Drew over her red, rectangular Chanel eyeglasses, her blue eyes widening.

"It didn't look like that from where *I* was standing," Madison said quietly, dropping her eyes to the floor. In that one dip of her head, Drew saw just how badly she was hurting, and something inside him softened a little bit. Shit, it was probably his fault anyway. Technically, he'd been leading her on, acting like he wanted to get back together, asking her out when deep inside he knew it would probably never really work between them. Drew stared at the way the soft light from the Japanese lanterns glinted off her shining hair, at her ridiculously lithe body underneath the tiny black dress she wore, at her perfect glowing skin and angular cheekbones—and he knew that he had to tell her that, if it had ever really started between them, it was now over. And he also knew that if he didn't suck it up and spit it out, he'd only hurt her again, and, more than anything, Drew was tired of hurting her. He was so tired of being the bad guy that he could barely breathe.

"Mad," he started, keeping his voice low so that the gawkers couldn't hear, "I know you're going to think I'm an asshole for doing this, and you'd be right—I probably am. But I'd be more of an asshole if I didn't say what I'm about to say." Madison raised her head, and when Drew saw the tears swimming around in her green eyes, he almost stopped himself. Drew took a deep breath and tried to find the right words, softening his voice to try to cushion the blow as best he could. "I think it was a mistake for us to try again. Maybe we're just not meant to be."

Madison flinched visibly, her face hardening like a mask, and for one split second, he wanted to take it all back and pull her to him—anything to stop her face from looking so totally disappointed and lifeless. She crossed her arms over her chest and looked away, blinking rapidly.

"If that's how you feel, then fine," she said, her voice wavering.

"It . . . is," Drew said tentatively. "And I'm sorry." Madison shook her head and turned around to face the street, her hair blowing gently in the breeze.

"Whatever," she said coolly, her tone level and steady now, as if by magic. "I'm over it—*and* you."

Drew flinched slightly at the ice coating her voice and reached out, his hand hovering above her shoulder for a few agonizing seconds before he came to his senses and pulled back. There was nothing he could do or say that would make her feel better right now—and Drew knew that if he touched her, or tried to give her a hug, she'd take it the wrong way. Hell, as pissed-off and hurt as she was, she might even punch him, and he knew from experience that Madison had a mean left hook. If she wanted to put him out, well, she could probably do it. Public humiliation was one thing, but he drew the line at getting slapped by a girl in front of two hundred of his closest friends. The only thing he could really do at this point was to walk away. He'd had enough practice at it, and this was one time where his skills would really come in handy. For the first time, he knew without a doubt, that there was really nothing left to say.

And with that, Drew turned to face the still-silent crowd, and walked slowly and deliberately inside to find Casey, turning his back on his past, and making his way, step by step, toward the future.

seven
minutes
in heaven

Casey sat on the edge of the Kohler freestanding
white soaking tub in the middle of the Van Allens' guest bathroom, staring down at her freckled, skinned knee, and wishing
she could just disappear. Who had she been kidding to think
that she could ever really fit in here? She looked around at the
gleaming black-and-white tiles, at the Swarovski crystal chandelier overhead that sprayed across the ceiling in the shape of
a branch dripping with crystal cherry blossoms, and sighed,
brushing away the hot tears falling from her gray eyes with the
back of her hand, not caring if she smeared her mascara everywhere. She'd only been in New York less than a month, and
already she'd ruined everything. The only thing that made her
feel even slightly better about the whole screwed-up situation

was the fact that she'd managed to tell Madison exactly what she thought—even if it hadn't made any real difference . . .

Casey looked down at the dress she'd loved so much a few hours ago, running her hands over the hopelessly wrinkled fabric, and sighed deeply as she grabbed a piece of toilet paper from the stainless steel dispenser and blew her nose, the sound echoing noisily off of the white walls. The dress that had made her feel like a princess a few short hours ago now hung loosely around her body like an old rag, like somebody's cast-off—which, of course, it was. Casey sighed, wondering how she was ever going to find the courage to leave the bathroom or face Madison ever again. And speaking of Madison, Casey was beginning to wonder if her whole life in Manhattan—assuming she even still had one after tonight—was going to consist of scooping up Madison's hand-me-downs. Would she always be second best, and in second place?

Casey jumped at the sound of a soft knock on the door. The knob began to turn, and the door opened, revealing Drew's tense, worried face. *Oh crap*, she thought, running her fingers under her eyes to try to reduce the racoonlike effect of her undoubtedly smeared mascara that probably made her look a hot mess. *Great. I'm in the bathroom crying, wearing his girlfriend's goddamn dress, and now he's probably going to tell me that he's getting back together with her*. She wondered just how much more humiliation she was going to have to endure this evening before she could sneak back to The Bram in shame and consume an entire pint of Häagen-Dazs chocolate-chocolate chip while watching bad reality TV until she passed out. Drew closed the door behind him with a sharp click, turning the lock. He walked over and sat down beside her on the side of the tub.

"Hey," he said, looking over at her. "I'm really sorry for what went down out there. Is your knee okay?"

"Yeah," she said quietly, wondering if it was completely obvious that she'd been bawling like an infant less than five minutes ago. Probably. "I'm okay. Its not your fault, anyway."

"Yeah, actually it kind of *is*," Drew said forcefully, and Casey turned to face him, completely confused. Drew exhaled heavily, turning and taking her hand in his. *Oh my God*, Casey thought, her heart beating crazily in her chest, *Drew Van Allen is holding my hand!* The sensation of his skin on hers was so warm and heady that she could barely concentrate on what he was saying. *Don't blow it this time*, her inner dating Nazi said coolly. *He probably just feels sorry for you.*

"I didn't know what I wanted for a while," Drew said quietly, running his fingers over hers with a light, delicate touch that made her want to jump out of her skin with excitement. Or hurl herself onto the white Flokati rug strewn across the tile floor at their feet and declare her undying love—either or.

"What about now?" Casey couldn't believe the words that were coming out of her mouth. Was she insane? Why was she in a hurry for him to tell her what she already knew—that he'd always been in love with Madison, that he still loved her.

"I know what I want now," Drew said, sinking to his knees on the white rug. "And it's you." Drew reached up, wiping away the tearstains from her face, and Casey threw her hands up in the air, blocking his touch.

"Why would you want *me*?" she asked. "I'm a total mess." *What are you* doing? her inner dating Nazi shrieked. *Are you trying to get rid of him?* Drew smiled, pushing her hands down and holding on to both of them with his own as he gazed up into her face, his lips turning up at the corners as he tried not to laugh.

"Then we're perfect for each other," Drew said, looking into her eyes. "I'm a mess, too. Besides," he added with a wink, "I think you're completely beautiful." He let go of her hands and gestured at her dress. "You could wear a paper *bag* and you'd still be beautiful." At those words, Casey's heart leapt in her chest, the word *beautiful* still ringing in her ears, and when Drew pulled her down off of the tub and into his arms, she wondered if her heart might actually stop altogether. *If I died right now,* Casey thought, closing her eyes, *it would be just fine with me.*

Drew leaned in, his lips grazing hers before they touched completely, his mouth opening under her own, electricity racing through her. The memory of every other boy she'd ever crushed on vanished in that one moment, until there was only Drew—his kisses both magical and perfect. The last time she'd made out with a guy was at a stupid kegger back home, where everyone was nostalgic for sixth grade. The night had deteriorated into rounds of Spin the Bottle, and an extended version of Seven Minutes in Heaven, where you macked on the cute guy of your choice for seven minutes in the nearest available closet. After a few lukewarm cups of beer, which made her feel slightly nauseous, she was pulled into a coat closet by Bobby

McFarlane for some face time, and he stuck his tongue down her throat like he was mining for gold. It was decidedly unpleasant—not to mention wet. But if kissing Bobby was seven minutes in hell, kissing Drew was more like seven minutes in *ecstasy*. When Drew finally pulled back, breathing quickly and pushing her curls out of her face with his fingers, Casey felt totally dazed, like she was sleeping deeply in a dream—the most wonderful, yummy dream she'd ever experienced. And if it really was only a dream, then she didn't ever want to wake up. Drew looked at her and smiled, his blue eyes shining, his dimple winking ecstatically.

"How about that tour of the city I promised you?" He took her hand in his own as he pulled her up, helping her off the floor. "Sometime this weekend, maybe?"

Casey stood up, nodding happily. Her butt was totally sore, her legs asleep, and there was a pack of vultures dressed head to toe in designer labels right outside the bathroom door. But despite all that, she was the happiest she'd ever been. She hadn't blown it after all—at least not with *Drew*. But she couldn't think about Madison now—not when Drew was staring into her eyes with that adorably kissable expression on his chiseled, gorgeous face. So she moved closer and did just that, twining her arms around his neck until Madison, Meadowlark, and the rest of the world fell away as he softly pulled her to him and leaned in for another kiss.

And now a special excerpt from the next book
in the Elite series . . .

IN TOO DEEP

Coming from Berkley JAM
October 2008!!!

Who's your
best friend?
Who's your
worst enemy?

One can never
really know . . . Enemy?
Who cares?
—Karl Lagerfeld,
Elle magazine,
September 2007

hot
lunch

Madison Macallister straightened the silken sleeve of her floral-patterned black-and-crimson Blumarine dress, and stabbed her fork into the desiccated remains of her smoked-salmon salad, bringing a forkful of baby greens and fish up to her matte, ruby-red lips. If she kept on eating this way, she was definitely going to blow up—and not in a good way. She was already changing into her baggy sweats the second she got home from school every day, and the waistband of her favorite new Citizens of Humanity jeans was decidedly snugger than when she bought them in a depression-fueled shopping incident a few weeks ago—a binge of Posh and Becks–worthy proportions that resulted in Edie storming into her room and cutting up her Amex Black card right in front of her. Madison exhaled deeply, spearing the last chunk of salty smoked fish and popping it into her mouth while checking out the six-carat square-cut emerald ring that shined brilliantly on her ring finger, winking in the fluorescent lighting. It had been worth it.

Besides, now that she was more miserable than ever, it seemed crucial to have a few things in her life that actually gave her pleasure—and shopping was definitely one of them. Drew Van Allen may have been history, but at least she had her new black leather Furla tote, trimmed in the softest gray fox fur *ever*, to console her. Madison was beginning to see that boyfriends came and went with alarming speed, and friends were clearly not to be trusted. But clothes? Clothes never let you down. And accessories were forever . . .

It'd been three weeks since Drew's party, three long, agonizing weeks when the leaves in Central Park first turned orange, then red, and began to crunch underfoot on the city streets. The nights grew progressively cooler, and more often than not, Madison found herself reaching for a cashmere sweater to throw over her shoulders in the early mornings, and pulling her caramel-colored Hermès riding gloves over cold hands that felt more like icicles than fingers. And even though the weather was definitely changing, things between her and Drew were not. Much like the first chilly days of winter—which were definitely now on the way—their relationship had completely frosted over. When they passed each other in the hall, Drew dipped his eyes away from her gaze and stared at the floor—especially if he happened to be walking with Casey. It had gone on for so long now that, even if for some bizarre reason they did end up talking again, she wouldn't have the faintest idea what to *say*. Somehow—at least for her, anyway—it was easier this way. Out of sight, out of mind—just like her credit card bills.

And if she wasn't thinking about the way he'd clearly dumped her for Casey, she didn't have to deal with the fact that he might just prefer someone else to her. But no matter how hard she tried, Madison just couldn't wrap her head around the idea. How was that even *possible*? And the only thing that even remotely put a crimp in her plans to pretend they'd both been inexplicably eaten by dinosaurs was the fact that she had to see the both of them every fucking day at school. And, worse yet, Drew didn't even seem to care—it was as if their entire past had been wiped out with the arrival of one frizzy-haired Midwestern freak with absolutely zero sex appeal, and who, despite her town of origin, was anything but "normal." Did the last two years mean nothing to him? Not only was this totally inconceivable, it was ruining her reputation! Everyone south of Park Avenue knew that Madison Macallister was the girl who got what she wanted—when she wanted it—and boys were no exception. Until now.

Adding insult to injury was the fact that it was the start of junior year, and that being said, not only was it time for sweater shopping at TSE's annual fall sale, but it was unfortunately also the beginning of endless amounts of prep courses, practice exams, and untold amounts of worrying about the upcoming SATs—not to mention the rapidly approaching nightmare of applying to colleges, and the enormous, looming, insurmountable question of what exactly she was going to do for the rest of her life. Madison didn't waste her time pondering these kinds of questions—mostly because she didn't have the first clue how to answer them. Choosing just one thing to do for the rest of your life seemed so . . . limiting. And limits were for tiny people with tiny minds—not for card-carrying members of the overprivileged set—who were supposed to have options as wide as the Atlantic.

But when it came right down to it, Madison wasn't exactly sure *what* it was that she was really good at in the first place—with the possible exceptions of gossiping and accessorizing. So, at parties, when the topic turned—as it inevitably did—to the future, Madison had made it a habit recently of smiling prettily—and then changing the subject so fast that her audience was left with a bad case of social whiplash. It was unthinkable. Madison Macallister, otherwise known as Ms. Perfect of the Upper East Side, without a plan? Not only could it destroy her reputation as the perfect Upper East Side robot princess, but it was also a potential embarrassment just waiting to happen. And Madison Macallister had made it a policy long ago to never, ever do embarrassing. If you were going to get all whiny and blubbery, you might as well just raise a white flag in the air, start wearing sweat pants to school, and just surrender what was left of your dignity. The very idea of it made her shiver, her tiny, ski-slope nose wrinkling in distaste.

"Look," Sophie whispered under her breath, diamond studs glinting in her honey hair, the majority of which was obscured by an Anna Kula gray tweed cap. "Check out the happy couple—major bonding at twelve o'clock," she added in a

conspiratorial fake-espionage voice. Even since *The Bourne Ultimatum* came out on DVD Sophie wouldn't shut up about spies and the CIA—not to mention Matt Damon's impressive arms in that gross, dirty green tank he wore for most of the movie.

And speaking of slightly crazier, fashion-obsessed wardrobes, in celebration of the newly crisp fall weather Sophie was wearing a pair of gray-wool Alexander Wang wide leg pants, and a white Alessandro Dell'Acqua silk blouse with an enormous loopy bow tied at the collar. An oversized leopard Jimmy Choo clutch sat on the table in front of her, and she absentmindedly stroked it while continuing to stare over Madison's head, her glossy pink lips parted. After years of being a veritable slave to Mystic Tan, Sophie had mysteriously halted her spray-tan obsession right after Drew's party with no explanation whatsoever, and as a result, her creamy skin glowed; her face rosy with just a hint of Benefit's Benetint rubbed onto the apples of her cheeks. Now that both Sophie and Phoebe were so scarily pale, Madison had taken to calling both of them the cadaver twins on account of the fact that they looked like they belonged in a fucking coffin.

As if she'd somehow read her mind, Phoebe raised her head from her iPhone and quit her incessant texting to glance across the room, her fingers halted on the keypad, her dark hair shining around her pale, heart shaped face as she sang along with Jay-Z and Rihanna as they blared through the Dining Hall's sound system. *You can stand under my umbrella . . . ella . . . ella . . . ella.* Rihanna sounded like she had an incurable—stutter—or a case of Tourette's. Not only was the song pathetically old but if she had to sit through it one more time she was going to stab herself in the eye with a fork. And if whatever spectacle going on behind her required actual movement, then it had better be good.

Madison stretched her arms over her head, and carefully turned around, her green cat eyes sweeping the crowded room, and settling uncomfortably on Casey and Drew, who were standing over at the coffee kiosk. Like they'd be anywhere else—Drew was so addicted to caffeine that there should've been a twelve-step program founded in his honor. Casey was wearing a faded pair of Seven jeans and a white sweater that looked like it came from some horrible suburban mall bargain basement. Even so, Madison had to admit that, as happy as Casey looked at that moment, it wouldn't have mattered if she were wearing a paper bag. Casey's cheeks glowed pinkly and her irrepressibly curly hair waved down her back in yellow curls that shone in the glaring overhead light. She was still the total definition of a hot mess though—albeit a *happy* hot mess. Drew, of course, was yummy perfection as usual—even though his dark hair fell into his eyes, obscuring them from view. Clearly it was time for a haircut, and the loose, white button-down Gucci shirt he wore was splattered with incipient coffee stains—Drew was nothing if not messy—but it didn't matter. He was still a vision in khakis. And as she watched Drew feed Casey a bit of a ginormous chocolate-chunk cookie, Madison felt like she was about to claw her way out of her own decidedly green skin.

"They really are kind of ridiculously cute together in a Saturday-morning-cartoons-and-Lucky-Charms kind of way,"

Phoebe said after noticing Madison's unbroken gaze toward the coffee kiosk.

"Lucky Charms make me want to vomit. Seriously," Madison said. She was having none of this cutesy bullshit.

"You don't like Lucky Charms?" Sophie practically screamed. "I LOVE Lucky Charms. I would always eat all the cereal bits first so the marshmallows would get all soft and the milk would turn purple . . ."

"ME TOO!" Phoebe squealed, interrupting her and then attacking her phone again as it beeped noisily.

"I'm not talking about cereal, dammit," Madison interrupted, trying to hold herself back from spitting her pent-up venom all over Sophie. "And who the hell are you texting anyway?" she snapped, pointing at Phoebe's phone. "We're practically your only friends." Phoebe's face turned crimson as she giggled nervously, shoving her phone into her oversized Tod's cream-colored tote that perfectly matched her ivory Calvin Klein wool pants and TSE cabled cashmere sweater.

"Well, we're the most *important* anyway." Sophie giggled, leaning over and sipping her iced hazelnut latte through a red plastic straw. "Did I tell you guys that we finally found a location for my party," Sophie said, her green eyes bright with excitement as she pushed her latte away and began absent-mindedly flipping though the pages of her cocoa-colored Hermès leather notebook she used to take notes in AP Algebra class. The pages were filled with neat mathematical diagrams in precise purple ink. "And, oh my God, it's going to be soooo amazing! Just last night I heard that . . ."

Madison sighed exasperatedly and turned away, staring off into space, the sounds of Sophie and Phoebe's incessant gossiping fading away like a bad radio signal. How could they not understand that what was going on in front of them was downright treasonous? In fact, it was an assault against all that the sovereign nation of Madison Macallister stood for. She had a mind to have Phoebe call Jason Bourne in to put a hit on the two for their crime against her. Or maybe there was another way . . .

Madison turned back to her empty plate and smiled as she pushed it away from her. She knew from experience that the best way to recapture a guy's interest was usually by getting interested in someone else, and Drew was definitely no exception. Besides, all guys were basically the same entity anyway—all they wanted was what they couldn't have. As soon as Drew saw her with another guy, he'd want her back all over again. She knew he'd start sending her flowers, showing up at her doorstep, basically groveling—and she was going to enjoy every ego-boosting minute of it.

Madison watched as Drew leaned in and gave Casey a long kiss good-bye, his hands on her shoulders, his fingers buried in her hair. Let him kiss whomever he wanted . . . now. By next week, she'd have a new boyfriend, and then he was going to be *really* sorry. Just the thought of her being interested in someone else would make him completely crazy—even if he didn't know it yet. And just because she got played didn't mean she had to sit around moping all year long, did it? Manhattan was a big city—and there were more than enough cute guys to distract her while she got this Drew problem ironed out. And with Drew out of the picture, the Casey situation would naturally take care of itself—before the fall term was over, her frizzy ass would be on a bus back to Nebraska, or wherever the hell she was from. *Count on it,* Madison thought as Casey tentatively approached the table, a bashful smile on her glowing, freckled face.

As much as it killed her to do so, Madison parted her lips and smiled back, remembering the advice her mother, Edith Spencer Macallister, had given her after Becca McCormick had the nerve to declare on the first day of fifth grade—and in front of the entire class—that Madison Macallister was a stuck-up little priss.

Keep your friends close and your enemies closer . . .

Make sure your beach bag is packed—grab these awesome Berkley JAM books!

How I Found the Perfect Dress

BY MARYROSE WOOD

After a summer full of time-travel, Morgan's back to her painfully normal life, until her friend, Colin, presents her with a problem. Faeries are forcing him to boogie with them for eternity, and now she has to break the spell and save him—all while finding the perfect prom dress...

The Elite

BY JENNIFER BANASH

When Casey McCloy moves to New York and joins the Upper East Side's social elite, she couldn't know the drama waiting for her—or the girl waiting to destroy her rep with one well-timed whisper.

The Guy Next Door

BY CAROL CULVER
(Available July 2008)

Maggie has always been a plain Jane, until the makeover of a lifetime gives her the tools she needs to make her move on the boy next door—but will she have the nerve to go for it?

Violet in Private

BY MELISSA WALKER
(Available August 2008)

After global jet-setting and flashing bulbs, Violet thinks she's ready to give up modeling and concentrate on college. But with Vassar so close to New York, modeling may not be ready to give up on *her*.

T30.0208